THE GOOD NAZI

The Good Nazi

D.A. Chadwick

WordMerchant Publishing

For my mother, Joyce Chadwick, who always wanted to see this story published when I first wrote it at age twenty as play. Hope she can see it from heaven.

1ˢᵗ Publication 2012 *The Good Nazi* by D.A. Chadwick
Second Printing, 2021 *The Good Nazi* *D.A. Chadwick*
ISBN 978-1-0878-8075-4

WordMerchant Publishing

Prologue

The convention hall at the Hyatt Hotel was packed with members of the Wichita Jewish Women's Association. They gathered to honor one of their newest members who had moved with her husband, Rabbi Herschel Levy from Chicago. After years of leading a large congregation he had decided to retire in the Midwest and teach Hebrew classes at the reform congregation of Temple Beth-El.

In Chicago, Ingrid Levy had been a pillar of the Jewish community, known for her passion for educating Jewish youth about their roots and continuing the ancient traditions of their faith. She organized fund raisings for libraries, museums, trips to Israel and had made substantial monetary contributions to Holocaust memorials across the United States. The last two years in Wichita had been no exception.

As the tall, silvery haired grandmother approached the podium, the audience stood and applauded the woman who had led a successful revitalization of the small Jewish community. At age eighty-five Ingrid was more active than most people half her age. She lived every day as if there would not be another, but that was a trait Ingrid shared with many Holocaust survivors.

She smiled sweetly, her gray eyes misting over at the warm response of women and men, as well as non Jewish people of Wichita, Kansas. Ingrid still had the bearing of a much younger woman, her voice still clear and strong as she began to address the audience.

The room was somewhat too warm and Ingrid pushed back her sleeves, revealing the number tattooed onto her left forearm by the SS at Auschwitz. There was an audible sigh as the crowd took in the significance. As she began her speech two men in dark suits entered the large room and approached the stage, their heavy footsteps pounding the carpet like knights on horseback. The taller one bounded up the steps and quickly stood next to her.

Rabbi Levy flew from his metal chair and demanded to know what they wanted. "Please, this is a very important event. Who are you?"

The shorter man identified himself as Agent Foster of the Kansas Bureau of Investigation. The one now handcuffing Ingrid Levy was Agent Largent. He told her she was under arrest for war crimes.

The rabbi and all the other spectators stood up, furious as the treatment of such a special community leader, but Ingrid's head dropped to her chest as she surrendered without a word of protest.

"Ingrid! What is this all about? Why are you arresting my wife! Has she not suffered enough from the Nazis?" The Rabbi tried to climb onto the stage only to have Foster pull him back.

As Ingrid was led by Agent Largent off the stage the defensive crowd demanded an explanation as to why someone who had survived Auschwitz was charged with war crimes.

Foster stopped for a moment and held up Ingrid's arm sporting the number. "Your concentration camp survivor failed to mention to immigration that she was a camp guard before pissing the Nazis off. Isn't that right Frau Brecht? "

The look of horror and confusion on her husband's face and on those of the other members of Temple Beth-El haunted Ingrid as she was escorted outside to the black unmarked car.

"How could you lie about such a thing?" Largent asked, struggling to control his anger as he pushed her head down under the car door frame.

"But I was an inmate at Auschwitz! I did not lie! You don't understand." Ingrid pleaded.

"Sure you were, I can dip a needle into some ink and give myself the same number. My grandmother lost her whole family to the camps, so do yourself a favor and shut the hell up." Largent scowled as Foster slammed the door on the old woman.

She glanced back at her husband and the people who had been her friends. Ingrid sobbed as the car pulled away. The past had crept up and shredded her heart and her life like a dagger.

One

Berlin

Spring 1938

"I'm flunking grammar; if I didn't need it to pass I wouldn't give a damn. I mean who really needs it anyway? Who has time to sit around writing besides monks and nuns!" Ingrid Brecht imitated a studious monk laboring over a manuscript.

She was tall, blond and gray eyed and the complete opposite of her long time friend, Anna Mendel, who was barely five feet and two inches from the ground and watched the changing world of Nazi Germany with serious dark eyes. They walked together every day after public school let out. Anna had recently left, no longer able to tolerate the horrid abuse of her Aryan classmates.

"Oh Ingrid, you can always make me laugh. You can make anything funny." Anna shook her head as the two turned down an alley." Mendel snickered; her faint little dimples showed for an instant then disappeared.

Brecht let out a deep breath. "I dread going home."

Anna stopped short, her face full of question. "Now what brought that on?" She pried into her friend with soft brown eyes, "cow eyes" Ingrid's stepfather had started calling them.

"My stepfather is shoving politics down our throats twenty-four hours a day. I can't stand it anymore. He's such a fat, disgusting oaf. We're near your father's store, that's what reminded me of him. I can't imagine why my mother married him. He blames everyone around him for his problems, now he includes Jews." Ingrid puffed out her cheeks and walked with a waddle.

Anna laughed at Ingrid then frowned thoughtfully. "It is just the times and your stepfather is no different from everyone out of work now. We Jews are to blame for everything you know. I'm sure we dropped off infected rats and caused the Black Death as well. It will pass Ingrid, it usually does. I won't be able to come home with you much longer though, he won't allow it."

The sterile appearance of the alley had Ingrid in another world. There was no trash in the clean little passageway, so uncluttered and clean unlike the city around them.

The girls were near John Mendel's pawn shop, a place where Ernest Brecht had gone many times to trade something of her mother's for booze money. John knew the woman's plight and tried to give as much as possible for the silverware or jewelry, hoping that some of the money would go for food. Ingrid's eyes widened when she processed Anna's words.

"No, he's just blowing and going with the crowd. He can't tell me what to do or who to see! You have nothing to do with any of Germany's mess."

Anna smiled sweetly. "Ingrid, you can be so naïve at times. Your father is pissed because he must get money from my father.

All he sees is that we have a business and he has no job. A Jew is a Jew, child or not. That Austrian, Hitler, is starting a career for himself by stoking the fires of anti-Semitism, which means anti-me! Funny thing is, we rarely ever go to the synagogue."

They emerged onto the street. "Now you sound like my father. You're both wrong about the Nazis in your own way. You'll see. I really think they will turn Germany around."

The atmosphere was full of electricity. A motorcycle whipped past, tossing their hair and skirts. The noise of the street was accompanied by a low hum and the sound of marching. People began to gather along the lane in anticipation.

Soon a mass of brown and red color rose in the distance, the hum slowly morphing into the chanting of male voices in unison. Ingrid stood at the curb to watch the men in uniform and could easily see above the crowd as the marchers in black pants and khaki shirts passed. They wore black leather belts with shoulder extensions and arm bands with swastikas. Scrubbed and clean shaven faces cast arrogant glances to the on lookers. Jack boots pounded the pavement as the young men moved down the road filled with mainly Jewish shops.

Anna lingered at the back of the crowd near a store front, pulling her sweater tightly around her. The Brown Shirts were the thugs of the National Socialist Party and were well known for vandalizing Jewish stores. It was clear from the look on Ingrid's face that the liveried young men were quite impressive to her. Ingrid motioned for Anna to come up closer, but Mendel shook her head and moved back further against the old walls.

Ingrid's shoulder's dropped and she pushed through the crowd to join Anna. "What's wrong with you? Don't they look grand?"

Anna's expression burned with disbelief. "Those charming boys are Hitler's demons who do his dirty work. Surely, your father has mentioned the Brown Shirts?"

"Of course he has and how can you believe the stories about them? Germany will be glorious again one day thanks to them." Ingrid beamed, trying to down play the feeling of foolishness that Anna could sometimes give her. Anna was suspicious of everything!

"Let's not talk here, okay?" Mendel could sense those near were listening.

"Hitler has already done great things for Germany. Every new leader has some problems to overcome. You know that, you're the good student not me." Ingrid winked to lessen the tension. She had loved Anna since they were toddlers, but the girl could see the devil in every shadow.

Anna walked back down the alley away from the crowd ogling the strutting Brown Shirts, her breast burning with anger and frustration. "You're my best friend, but at times I want to strangle you! Ingrid, you seem to stick your head in the sand and see nothing that goes on around you. Don't let the world pass you by, especially not now. You have to be aware!"

"I know, I know. I promise to pay more attention." Ingrid felt like she would forever be the school girl being chastised by the teacher. Her face was drawn, a familiar sign of pouting. She turned back to glimpse the last of the Brown Shirts and one man winked at her, bringing a blush to her creamy cheeks. "I will learn more about them." She smiled.

When Brecht turned back Anna was half way down the alley in the opposite direction. "Anna!" She ran to catch up and grabbed the other girl's arm. "Where are you going? I thought you had to help your father out today?"

"I do, but I'll go around. I'll not mingle with that lot." A gust of wind brought the scent of baking bread down the passage. A sudden hunger pang made Ingrid eager for dinner. The crowds cheered as young women threw flowers at the dashing men in uniform, making Ingrid want to run back and join them. She was irritated at Anna's attitude. Why go home when others their age were involved in such fevered activity?

Maybe her stepfather was right? Anna could be a stick in the mud at times. Ernest had often said that the only ones in Germany with money were Jews; everyone else had to scratch out a living. It was true that Anna always got her way and she certainly was clever, but could little Anna and her family really be undermining the future of the fatherland? If Anna loved Germany, then why did she so criticize the government? Anna stood on the street at the opposite end of the alley and shouted for Ingrid to hurry up if she was coming.

Brecht broke into a graceful jog and quickly caught up with the shorter girl, her gold braids bouncing with every stride. "You don't have to get snippy." Ingrid retorted, slightly winded.

"Are you mad because I didn't stay and watch?" Mendel asked with her right hand placed on her hip as she often did when the answer was already apparent. Anna did not enjoy bossing Ingrid around; Ingrid just let her take the lead. There was nothing stopping her from remaining with the crowd and flirting with the Brown Shirts.

"Why is very thing I like stupid or foolish and everything you like the proper thing?" Ingrid walked next to Anna, her face pointed to the pavement as she scraped the soles of her shoes on the bricks.

They walked for another block then turned down another alley to their right. John Mendel's shop was directly opposite the mouth of the passage at the far end.

"We'll have a good discussion about politics soon, Ingrid and I'll try to explain why I don't like the current events, but I really have to help my father out today. It's always the busiest near the end of the month."

"You think I don't understand anything and that I can't make up my own mind!" Ingrid retorted like a scolded child.

Anna smiled patiently. "I'm sure you can Ingrid, but you always seem easily influenced by those around you. Me included, I know." She hugged her pouting friend. "Look Brecht, I'm not blind. I know what you see in those dashing young men and their smart uniforms. They do look sharp and powerful, but that is the whole point isn't it? It's no accident that the Nazi party is the second largest in Germany now."

"My youth group is okay. We don't do anything political you know. I love the sports and being outdoors." Ingrid asked, not really wanting to hear the answer since she loved the League of German Girls.

The other girl reflected for a moment. Anna had no use for the Nazi youth groups, which pounded Nazi ideals into their members. The Brown Shirts were recruited from the Hitler

Youth and they were a brutal lot. Not wanted another argument, Anna replied. "Enjoy your friends; you must live in these times after all." She wondered what life would be like if she were on the "right" side. Would she still find the Nazis so objectionable?

When they arrived at Mendel's Pawn Shop, the two girls parted ways and Anna entered the store. Anna paused then shouted, "And tell your father I said hello." Ernst Brecht would not find it very funny as he liked Anna less every day. Shortly, her presence around the Brecht household would be a thing of the past and, she suspected, Ingrid's friendship.

John Mendel was a man in his sixties with a large gray mustache and round, gold glasses. He was giving Mrs. Gardner a few marks for a painting when he heard his daughter enter. She was the recent widow of a lawyer whose pension had been made void by the Nazi government. Anna nodded to her father then went to the file box on the wall for the day's receipts, which were over flowing. If her father did not stop helping the poor around them the Mendel's would soon join them.

Anna watched Ingrid walk back down the alley through the storefront window. She was the epitome of the Aryan image and would do well in this regime; Nordic perfection without even trying. Soon Anna suspected they would not be hanging out together at all.

The Nazis had already instituted a quota of Jews in the public schools and her little five year old niece would not be allowed to enter German public schools. Of the new school applicants only 1.5 percent could be Jews. Little Sarah Rosen was not one of them. Anna had been an exception since her father was a WWI veteran, but the terrible treatment of "non-Aryan" students had forced her to leave and attend a Jewish school.

Mrs. Gardner smiled and nodded to Anna as she passed. At least the woman could buy a few groceries now.

"Papa, do we have any money in the register?" Anna inquired as she leaned on the counter.

"We have enough to live and that is what counts yes? How can I not help who I can? These people have been our neighbors for years." John tilted his head; his warm eyes had always reminded Ingrid of Santa Claus. "Benjamin lost several patients today, all arrested and taken off by the Gestapo."

Anna frowned. Benjamin Rosen was her brother-in-law, a physician. "Why? Soon there will be no young Jewish men in Berlin outside the camps." Everyday more and more Jewish men were arrested and drug off to camps like Dachau and Oranienberg built because the jails could not hold all the new criminals of the Third Reich.

"Who knows with those brutes? Jewish doctors have few enough patients since losing the national health insurance coverage and then being banned from treating Aryans. He still has some patients, but there may be problems getting drug prescriptions filled. Jews can no longer practice pharmacy in Germany."

"Why don't we leave! This humiliation is going to get worse, I know it." Anna's heart burned with youthful fury.

"Now Anna, this is our home. Mama and me, as well as our grandparents, were born here. We're Germans. I fought in the war. I don't want to leave my homeland. I'm sure this will blow over, dear. Jews have always been a convenient political scapegoat." John took her hands and squeezed them.

She cleared her throat and suddenly felt hopeless. "I hope you are right, but I fear that the worse is yet to come."

"I understand your reservations about being here. Ingrid's father was in here this morning. He was very angry that I could not give him much for an old hunting rifle." Mendel chuckled. "It was such a piece of junk! It could hardly be called a gun."

"I don't go over to her house anymore. Mr. Brecht hates me and watches my every move." Anna took the receipts over to a small desk to one side of the store and began to add the amounts. She hung her heavy coat on the back of an old chair.

John looked out the store front windows and watched snow begin to fall. "Isn't it funny how snow can make everything seem fine? It cleans and muffles the chaos."

Anna was lost in her own thoughts as the snowflakes became larger. Everyone and everything was changing, growing old all of a sudden. She was no longer seventeen and could not remember a time when she had the carefree thoughts of a child. Anna was more sensitive to her surrounding than most of her peers, especially Christians like Ingrid who could not care less about political leaders and their agendas.

Ingrid had nothing to fear except drowning in the propaganda that flooded the streets. She would believe whatever she was told, not at first maybe, but sooner or later the message would sink in. Ingrid Brecht would make a dangerous enemy with the stubborn, cruel streak that had begun to expose itself more frequently. It would raise its head when she was hurt, embarrassed or angry. With the fevered atmosphere, Ingrid would be hell to be around, but Anna still loved the extroverted blonde haired girl who could every bit as sweet as she could mean. They had been friends since early childhood and she hated to think of a time when they might be enemies. It was probably inevitable.

The shop was busy as it always was when the economy was poor and Anna dreaded it. When her father was a success, it meant that other people were not. Men in work clothes came in with heads down and fists clenched. What hard earned possession would they give up that day? It was a time of stress and resentment.

It was not that Anna disliked the lending trade, but being Jewish and a money lender was a bad combination. She had felt the pressure at school when the other students noticed that Anna always had good shoes, never did without lunch and her father was not out of work. Hitler must be right about Jews as everyone in Germany was suffering except them.

She sometimes wished that John Mendel had a factory job like Ernest Brecht. They might be poor, but they would also be much less hated and less noticeable. When some of the customers would look at Anna she could feel their humiliation and shame as once she had spent the night with their daughters and ate meals in their homes.

Such times made Anna want to seek out other religions. It was a thought that she would not share with her parents as they would be hurt, however, it was an idea that dwelled in the back of her mind with the ever increasing fear that terrible times were ahead in Germany.

Growing up she had been taught that Jews had always suffered, but she heard it with indifference the way all children listen to past woes-it did not apply to her. Now Anna felt that she was destined to live the trials of her ancestors that would soon be in full bloom. The seeds were in the faces of her friends, of people in the neighborhood and the fearsome sound of jack-boots pounding the streets.

The little gold bells tingled as the last customer left the shop. John Mendel held paper bills in his hands behind the counter. He opened the cash register and placed the money in a lock box. "So, my little bookkeeper, how was your day?" He patted his nearly empty cash box.

"It was fine, nothing unusual or exciting." She smiled back. Anna was a practical, logical person whose emotion rarely played with her features. Her father did not notice that she was still disturbed by the seeing the parade of storm troopers earlier.

"Think we will take the books home tonight and do them. I've been working late every night this week and it upsets your mother. You know how she is about her suppers!" He went through a curtain that mussed his hair to lock the rear entrance.

Anna could hear him push the door shut tight and slide the bolt into the latch. The way he came back through the curtains reminded her of an actor doing an encore. John Mendel was such a quiet, gentle man and the world around him was becoming very harsh. She was afraid for him and her mother, Ilse. They would take much before fighting back, if they ever would. "Yes, Momma doesn't like us to work so hard."

He scanned the interior of the store to ensure every item was still in place as some shop lifting had occurred lately. Anna grabbed her father's light gray fedora and the knit sweater given to him for his birthday from the coat rack near the door. John

Joseph Mendel, with sweater pulled on, closed and secured the shop while his daughter patiently waited.

Anna was not a beauty who would find a husband based on her looks, and men generally did not want a woman smarter than themselves. He was not sure what the future held for Anna, but he could not see her being content to burp babies and bake bread.

His first born, Helene, was a good looking girl who had married a fertile young doctor and already had borne him five children. Bernard and Helene took the command to "Go forth and multiply" very seriously. John laughed to himself then caught Anna's questioning look as they walked down the street. He winked and squeezed her shoulder. Anna was so different from her sister Helene who was out going and possessed a natural instinct for motherhood. She would always be happy with her husband and children, feeling fulfilled by her duties to them with no need to argue politics, but Anna! She always had her nose in a book and some opinion on whatever the issues were at the time.

Anna was not ugly by any means, but her beauty was not explosive. It emerged as one got to know her, listened to her speak and looked into her brown eyes. She had an intriguing grace that blossomed as friendship grew. In many ways his little shopkeeper was the true beauty of the family.

After walking for two blocks the street filled with colorful leaflets bearing the swastika of the *National Socialist Workers Party*, also known as the Nazi party. There was graffiti on the sidewalks and buildings slanting Jews. Mendel stooped to retrieve one of the pamphlets. "What kind of nonsense went on there today?" He asked the vacant street as snow swirled about them.

Anna took a deep breath and let it out somewhat sorrowfully. "There was a parade of Brown Shirts this afternoon, Ingrid and I saw them."

He crumbled the paper in his fist and tossed it into the gutter. "They make us out to be the Anti-Christ! What is becoming of our city?" He demanded.

Taking his arm, Anna guided him toward their apartment a few blocks away. "It's just more propaganda, Papa." She tried to comfort him as she often did because he took things so personally. The cruel remarks would bother him for the rest of the evening. Not that Anna enjoyed being called names or blamed for the failure of others; she just did not let it cut her to the heart. The less information you gave someone, the less damage they could inflict and the harder it was to cripple you.

A cold breeze whipped down the lane, making the striped awnings flap and snap in the wind. The sun had surrendered the sky over to yellowish gray clouds that hung heavy above Berlin, making the air seem colder that it really was.

John cleared his throat. "You know, Anna, people that I have known for many years are coming to me for money. They bring their prized belongings and wait nervously, trying to avoid looking at me while I decide what I can give them. I wish they would go to someone they do not know. It would not be so degrading. He adjusted his hat, which had slipped sideways. "Some of them hate me, Anna, because I cannot give them more. They are out of work and they blame me." The slight man blinked and squeezed his lips together.

While searching her brain for a response, Anna heard voices and scuffling in the sound of pounding feet in the alley they had just passed. Her heart skipped a beat and a wave of terror came rushing up from deep inside her. Mendel stared at his daughter wide-eyed and she returned the stare only long enough for him to grab her arm and pull her across the street. Anna glanced back to catch the toothy grins of three Brown Shirts, collars open, uniforms wrinkled with a look of drunkenness. The father and daughter ran faster hoping to get back to the store and slip inside.

One of the men fell. The other two stumbled back to help him up, their laughter bouncing off the brick walls and further scaring the fleeing Jews. The older man and the girl ducked into a passageway. The black haired man who had tripped tossed an empty bottle into the street where it smashed to pieces. It angered him to have an old man and a girl evade him and his friends.

"Gruber! Circle the block and meet them at the other end. Franz and I will chase them from this end." He commanded in a strong, clear voice that was eagerly obeyed. He was taller than his companions and appeared older as he brushed the dirt from his pants.

Anna bumped into a row of trash cans near the middle of the dark alley. "Come, we have to hurry!" Her father urged, out of breath and holding his side. She stood up, gritting her teeth at the pain in her shin. They raced for the street as fast as their tired feet would allow. Anna saw the red bricks fly pass in a blur and the ground below her was a mass of color from trash cans knocked over in the alley.

Suddenly something hit her hard from behind and then someone held her tight. When her mind cleared she focused on the beige buttons and rumpled black neck tie of a Brown Shirt not much taller than her. His blue eyes and light brown sideburns framed a wide smile with a chipped tooth.

"Why nobody told me little Jewish whores could be so pretty, soft brown eyes and such nice lengthy locks." The man ran a hand through Anna's hair while talking in a sing-song voice.

She leaned forward away from him and he tightened his grip. Looking back, she saw the name, Holtz on his name tag. He punched her in the kidneys making Anna groan in pain. When he pulled her against him she felt a bulge in his pants.

"Get your filthy hands off me!" Anna screamed, twisting violently around. She brought a knee sharply into his swollen groin. Holtz let go and

with watering eyes stepped backward and fell hard on his buttocks.

The other two men had caught her father. One was holding him while the black haired one punched him in the stomach and face. She snatched up a piece of brick, heaving it like a missile. It left a deep gash in the attacker's forehead. Anna ran over to her father and took his out stretched hand. He looked bad and he too old for this sort of beating. By that time people walking by began stopping and staring at the action in the alley.

"Come Papa, we need to go home." Anna glared at the uniformed men.

Uncomfortable with the extra attention, the black haired man waved a fist at the escaping Jews. The name on his tag was

Swartz. "You'll regret this you little bitch! You can't treat us this way. Schwein, schumtz! "

The three Brown Shirts retreated licking their wounds, glaring at their retreating prey with eyes like burning coals, yelling profanities and spitting on the ground. The sense of dread that Anna had lived with before was now overwhelming. It was the first real terror she had ever known.

Two

1938

Berlin

Ingrid Brecht sat in the hot classroom barely hearing the low, droning voice of the teacher writing on the blackboard. The school's old boiler worked too well and was doing a superior job of roasting the students. Every so often she would have to peel away the skirt that plastered itself to her skin, which would then stick to the wooden seats.

The subject was world history, of which Ingrid has no interest at all, finding it unbelievably boring. Ironically, Anna loved it, but could no longer attend classes with her. They had to settle for meeting after school at the Tiergarten. She needed to speak to her friend who had been moody; no hostile was a better word. When they had passed in the street Anna had only mumbled a greeting, but when Ingrid looked into her brown eyes she felt as if she had done Anna some wrong. The girl was prone to moodiness, but this time was different. Something had happened to her.

"What? Sir, could you repeat the question?" Caught daydreaming again, he repeated the question and her response was wrong. Herr Krause ought to know by now that whether Ingrid listened or not her answer would be incorrect. Someone across the room raised his hand bringing a smile to Krause's face. The teacher was always thrilled to have students actually interested in his class, though every subject now was tinted with Nazi ideals.

The clock on the wall seemed to be moving in slow motion. Ingrid tried to focus on the blackboard, but her mind was on her troubled friend. Who could concentrate in this heat anyway? The room had windows with all of the casements on that side of the building facing a brick wall that hindered any passing breeze. A bead of sweat ran down the side of her face as if to mock the pitiful efforts of a small black fan in the corner.

The bell rang. It sounded more like something in a fire station than a school building. Ingrid jumped. Finally! Now she would find Anna but she was also somewhat worried about talking to Anna when she was angry. The coolness that surrounded the girl when she was upset frightened Ingrid, even though living with Ernst Brecht she had learned how to handle anger expressed with cursing, fists and furniture throwing.

Anna was different from most people Ingrid knew; smart, logical and mature for her age. Ingrid's concerns always seemed so petty compared to the important issues churning through Anna's mind. At the risk of pushing Anna further away and bridling what little emotion she showed, Ingrid would try to find the cause of her moody demeanor.

Several large boys pushed through the threshold ahead of her, knocking Ingrid hard into some lockers. Some of the papers in her arms fell to the floor and scattered.

"Why the hell don't you watch where you're going?" She snapped, her golden hair hanging in her face as she knelt to pick up her notes.

The boys who had bumped into her snickered as they half-heartedly apologized. Ingrid rose to her full height, glaring in their direction. She towered over them. The larger of the two, Heinz Gruber, motioned for his buddies to leave her alone, but it provoked a negative response.

The shortest one poked Ingrid and laughed. "I think Heinz is like his big brother, right? You and Franz would both like to know Ingrid a little better!"

Gruber grabbed the boy's shirt collar and jerked him down the corridor, mumbling to him through gritted teeth. Ingrid Brecht gave her head a toss, flipping a lock of hair out of her eyes. She let out a disgusted breath then turned and walked briskly down the hall in the opposite direction.

She passed the locker that used to be Anna's and felt a twinge of sadness that their school days together were over. Ingrid then hurried out the front doors to hit all of Anna's haunts when not at her father's shop. The library and several bookstores proved futile, so Ingrid pushed past the crowds on the sidewalks toward Mendel's Pawn Shop.

When she approached the alley near the store, a racket arose from the passage. Ingrid peered around the corner and spotted Anna kicking trashcans and throwing the spilled contents at the walls. Ingrid was stunned and stood there for several seconds. She had never seen Anna behave in such a manner and approached slowly as if walking on eggshells.

"Anna, what are you doing?" Why didn't you wait for me? When her friend did not answer Ingrid continued. "Well, the least you could do is acknowledge me!"

The small framed girl almost looked like some wild imp from the forest with her hair mussed and her foul mood twisting her features. "Ingrid, you are concerned the way you usually are! If my behavior disturbs your routine, then it's a problem." Anna felt her rage subside slightly, vented through icy words and tossed trash bins.

They stood facing each other until Anna broke the uneasy silence. "Sorry, for jumping all over you. I'm just so damned mad!" She had hurt Ingrid and Anna knew that it would take much sweet talking to ease the tension. No matter what Anna might be experiencing she always ended up take care of Ingrid.

Anna had to admit that she both envied and resented the carefree lifestyle and attitude of Ingrid's existence. She never had to worry about cold realities, the kind that hunted down old men and young girls as they headed for home.

The memory of her father being held by those goons and beaten had plagued Anna through the night and all day. They had never known such poor treatment before; being chased, taunted and hit like common ruffians. With all her heart Anna wished that she could bury her face in Ingrid's shoulder and sob, for once not have to be the strong one.

"What happened to you Anna?" Ingrid's eyes were the same blue as her sweater and could wring the truth out of the most stubborn person.

"You remember those grand looking young Brown Shirts?" Anna paused as Ingrid cocked her head like it would aid in her understanding the event. "Papa and I ran into three of them so rummy they couldn't stand up. The brain washed fools! They hunted us down like stray dogs." Anna's voice rose with anger. "We were not bothering anyone, just going home. She swallowed a lump that was forming in her throat. "We ran but they caught us and they beat my father."

Ingrid watched Anna force back tears that welled in her brown eyes. "How is he? Did they hurt you?" Ingrid wanted to comfort her best friend, but feared that Anna would not want her to push too far or be too physical. Anna was not the overly affectionate type.

"No, they didn't get the chance, but I know what they had in mind for me." Anna's stomach turned as she recalled the erection of her captor. "Papa stayed home today, he's very sore and bruised. Mendel's shop was rarely ever closed except for the Sabbath and religious holidays. There was something dark and unsettling about this forced day off that seemed like a bad omen.

"I'm so sorry, Anna. I never dreamed those men would want to hurt you, at least it's over." Ingrid spotted a coin on the pavement and bent over to grab it.

Anna's soft brown eyes looked tired as she shook her head. "No, it's only the beginning. They are not going to leave us in peace; things will get much worse before it is all over."

Ingrid searched her mind for something to say that would ease her friend's pain. It made Ingrid ache to think of anyone treating the Mendel's so badly. A kinder family one could never hope to meet, though Ernst Brecht tormented her more and more regarding her friendship with Jews.

Her stepfather had even implied that Anna was a lesbian, a pervert out to seduce his daughter. Ingrid had read some books in the library about such women who were supposed to ape the behavior of men and were very unhappy. Anna did not seem to fit the description.

Once Ingrid and her older brother, Albert, had sneaked across the railroad tracks to the tenements near the station house where he pointed out a figure standing near one building. He giggled as the short, stout woman brushed something off her trousers. *She's wearing men's clothes?* Ingrid had wondered aloud. Albert shook his head in confirmation. He said that some of them wore men's clothes and some did not. Ingrid had stared at the lone woman for some time then slowly brought her eyes back to her brother. He smiled, cocked his head toward the stranger and told his sister that the woman liked to have sex with other women. A sharp stab penetrated her heart at the thought.

Ingrid had always enjoyed playing house with Anna and their other girl friends. Because of her height Ingrid had usually played the father figure. She had relished kissing Anna as she arrived home from "work". Albert said that women who make love to women cut their hair short and have fat asses, which horrified Ingrid. She vowed then to conceal such affection for Anna from her stepfather.

They walked together silently until near the Brecht apartment, not wanting to say goodbye yet, Ingrid asked Anna to come home with her. "Can you come up for moment?" She squeezed Anna's arm. "Please, you have some spare time don't you?"

Anna sighed and looked to the gray sky above. "Your father doesn't want me around."

"You've been coming home with me for years, Anna. He can't rule me, just my mother." Ingrid stated firmly.

Anna heard the disgust in her friend's voice over Brecht. He was abusive and controlling and Anna could remember a time when he was not around.

Ingrid wondered how Anna could sense the smallest change in someone. Ernst had always been a prick, but Anna was right that he was changing and becoming more hateful and mean. It was true that he was nagging more at the dinner table about the money-grubbing Jews. He criticized Anna, but not to her face. Around her he was always polite. She suspected that Ernst was intimidated by the intelligent girl.

"For a short time, and only because I don't want him to control me either." Anna grinned slyly. She also hoped that Brecht would ignore her, or better yet, not be home. He hated Anna because all Jews were financial wizards and he was a financial flop.

The stairway to the second story apartment was narrow and not very well lit, but it was kept tidy and painted periodically. Ingrid turned to the wooden door left at the top of the stairs and opened it. The smell of cabbage, tomatoes and sausage rushed out and tinted the air in the hallway.

"Mom is making stew." Ingrid said to her friend, though the explanation was not necessary. It was one of Anna's favorites at the Brecht house.

Gretchen Brecht stirred the mixture in a deep pot and smiled when she saw it was the two girls and not her husband."How was your day girls?"

"It was boring and hotter than hell." Ingrid replied as she peered into the pot.

Her mother smacked her on the shoulder. "Watch your mouth! How are you Anna? We have not seen you for some time."

Anna liked the tall, stout woman whose light brown hair had just a trace of gray. Mrs. Brecht had always been kind to her and Anna enjoyed talking with her. "I'm doing fine, thank you. You are looking very well, Mrs. Brecht."

"Thank you Anna! Are you keeping up with your studies?" Gretchen asked while wiping her hands on an embroidered towel. She had been sorry to see Anna leave the public high school.

"Yes, Ingrid brings me daily assignments and the Jewish school is helping me to pass the Arbiter. I have hopes of entering the university someday to study medicine, though the competition is very tough."

Ingrid bit into an apple and went down the hall to her bedroom. Anna followed with Mrs. Brecht saying that she knew that Anna would go far in life.

After turning on the radio, Ingrid flopped on the bed and put her hands behind her head. "You're so smart; you should have been their child. They think a college education is the ultimate in achievements. Something I'll never give them. They wanted brains but all they got is beauty!" Ingrid struck a sexy pose then broke out laughing.

Anna surveyed the golden hair, sparkling gray eyes and long slender legs. "You got the looks and I got the brains, together we make the perfect daughter! My mother would rather have had a beautiful baby factory than a bookworm, so maybe we should trade places? " She crept onto the edge of the bed beside Ingrid who leaned over to pull something out from under the bed.

Ingrid grinned at a curious Anna. "Albert gave me this, but don't tell anybody I have it. My mother doesn't think its lady like." It was a boxing magazine.

Anna appeared puzzled. "What do you know about boxing? You've never mentioned anything like that before."

Ingrid flipped through the pages. "I just think I'd like to see a fight some time. In fact, I think I'd like to try it." She laid the book in her lap and began

to punch the air. She bit her lip, and then smiled at Anna. "You think I'm nuts, right?"

Anna read a caption under a black and white photograph of a man posed in a fighting stance. "No, I just haven't seen this side of you before. I never have heard of female boxers. Why didn't you tell me?"

Ingrid shrugged with a mellow expression, her lip curling slightly in a foolish grin. "Well, I thought you would think I was stupid."

"I don't think you're stupid. There's something that I want to do after I graduate from college. I want to learn to fly." Anna giggled. "Don't know why really, but I need to see the world from up there."

Ingrid tossed the magazine to the foot of the bed. She patted Anna's hand. "I should have known you wouldn't laugh at me.

I don't see anything wrong with wanting to be a pilot either." The image of a masculine Anna in aviator's glasses and a leather jacket made her grin.

Anna suddenly wondered when Ernst Brecht was coming home. "I don't want to be here when he gets back."

The muscles in Ingrid's jaw flexed as she tried to remove some object from her teeth. She knew where her stepfather was, as did her mother. The past few months Ernst had been spending his time at a nearby bar, and not entirely for drinking purposes. After a night with the boys, he came home full of ideas, some good, some bad, but what scared Ingrid was he did not always come home smelling of booze. Something had become more important to him than alcohol.

The bars were filled with large groups of middle-aged fathers and young men crowded into smoked clogged rooms, all patting each other on the back to the tune of some outraged orator. Brecht would come home assuring his wife that Germany would be fine once the Jews were taken care of-there lie the solution to an ailing fatherland.

About the time that Ernst began being interested in politics, he also started dragging his wife and stepdaughter to church, although they had never attended services regularly before. Ingrid was not very concerned with the sudden interest in religion, but the ranting about Jews as Christ-killers sent a chill down her spine.

"Oh he won't be back for hours. He's downtown with his pals." Ingrid replied, not wanting to elaborate on the subject. She felt Anna's deep brown eyes on her and felt like a traitor.

Anna nodded. She knew where Herr Brecht was spending his time since being unemployed. She had known by his change in attitude that he had been hanging out at taverns, swigging warm beer, smoking cigars and hashing out the fate of Germany. It was time to blame the Jews again. Yes, let's hear it. Rah, rah let's torment the Jews and all will be well! Funny, then that when things were going good the Jews got no credit for it. She looked over at Ingrid who appeared guilt ridden.

"Ingrid, I know what sort of things your father says about me. You don't have to protect me."

Suddenly embarrassed, Ingrid's cheeks turned pink and she jumped off the bed. "Please, I'm not 'protecting' you!" In truth, Ingrid was afraid, afraid that the Mendel's would move out of Germany and she would lose the one true friend she had. Ingrid wished that she was the kind of person who could be affectionate and tell people that she loved them, but the Brecht's were not that sort, not that Anna was either.

"I just don't want you to think that I agree with my stepfather's opinions. I don't understand everything the way you do, I'm not that smart and I know it. There is some bad talk out there and I'm scared that something will happen to you."

Anna smiled and walked over to the taller girl who fiddled with her fingernails. "They don't hate me or my family personally. Everybody needs something or someone to point the finger at, for now it is Jews." She let a sigh. "Times are hard and are getting worse. It helps people to think there is a cause for their suffering and it gives them direction."

The light in the room had darkened as the sun sank into the horizon. Ingrid's face was full of deep shadows and against the gray-green walls resembled some painter's haunting portrait. The set jaw, cool gray eyes and the thin mouth, Ingrid was naturally sensual. Anna pushed back the desire that was rising in her, never dreaming that her friend fought a similar battle.

Mrs. Brecht knocked softly on the bedroom door and told them dinner was on the table. Ingrid reached behind her to grab the door knob. "You will stay and eat with us, won't you?" She asked, peering down from her six-foot frame.

Anna bid her to lead the way. Something told her to accept the invitation because if this was not the last visit, it was next to the last.

The meal was a simple, meatless stew with homemade bread. The three women chatted, but the atmosphere was tense as none of them knew when Ernst Brecht would return home and just what sort of mood he would bring with him. He would be furious that there was no sausage in the stew, though one could not tell as the odor of cooking sausage had been absorbed by the wall paper and the old furniture, reminding Anna of a butcher shop.

Three

1938

Berlin

"John, you're not going to the shop today, not so soon?" Ruth Mendel looked pleadingly at her husband who sat on a kitchen chair tying his shoes. She was a plump woman and her modest dress strained at the seams.

Mendel straightened up, shaking his head. "You would have me home everyday if you had your druthers!" He winked at her. "As it is, I've had one many days off." The thin, gray haired man went into the living room to retrieve his hat and coat from a closet.

Ruth began to clear the table of breakfast dishes. She was worried not only about his existing wounds, but those she feared he might receive in the future. Those men could be waiting for him on the street's somewhere and they would not let him slip away a second time. He would go off to work as though nothing had happened as would Anna. The two of them were just alike and just as stubborn.

Deep down, Ruth wanted to pack up and leave Germany like many of their friends and relatives were doing, but John would not hear of it. Not John Joseph Mendel-Germany was his country and he would not be forced out. It was her country too, but Ruth had the same dreadful feeling about the days to come.

Anna entered the kitchen with her arms full of books. An unemployed teacher, Hansel Keller, now instructed many of the Jewish children in the neighborhood since they could no longer attend public school. She would have lessons until noon and then go help her father at the shop.

"I'm going now. I want to get there a little early." A night filled with demonic Brown Shirts had robbed Anna of any sleep.

"Anna, you look terrible! When you get home this afternoon you're not going to do anything but rest. Do you understand me? Frau Mendel frowned seriously at her daughter. "You and those books! They won't do you any good when raising children." She tapped the volumes with the end of her finger.

Herr Mendel returned and pointed his pipe at his wife. "Leave her be, mother. Anna's a smart girl who gives us no trouble!" He shooed her out the back door.

"Do you want me to walk with you to work, Papa?" Anna asked, protectively.

"No, I think I will ride my bicycle today." He replied, taking in a lungful of cool, Berlin air.

"You foolish old man! Your ribs are still sore, maybe even cracked, but who knows since you won't go to the doctor, and already you want to ride that contraption." Ruth straightened her apron, trying muffle a smile.

"Anna, your mother is all talk, talk, talk! Let's get out of here already." He pulled his hat down over his forehead and grabbed a sweater from the coat rack near the kitchen door.

They closed the door behind them. Anna grinned broadly, which did not escape her father's attention.

Peering over his gold-framed glasses he inquired while mounting his bike, "What is it you find so amusing might I ask?"

"You and Mama, you two are so funny." Anna's pushed her hair back out of her eyes as the wind gently tossed it. Her parents talked to each other that way most of the time, making everyone around them laugh.

"Your mother is right though, Anna. You don't look well." John peddled slowly along beside her. "Is there something wrong?" His young daughter shook her head, but he was not satisfied.

"It's as though you bury your head in books to hide from something. Am I right?"

The dark-haired girl blinked. There was something wrong, but she could not tell him or anyone else. Her father often took up for her on the subject of marriage when her mother would nag at Anna about prospective grooms. He also understood her lack of interest in having children, but her father really had no concept of what was bothering Anna.

How could Anna discuss what she did not understand? In truth she did want to marry, but the only person who had ever made Anna feel that way was Ingrid. How could she describe the loneliness and isolation she felt every single day? Frustration was the sort of her insomnia, and doubts about what sort of future she had with such feelings.

"I'm just tired, Papa." Tired of hiding, tired of hurting and tired of the terrible uncertainty of the times, she thought.

The merchants along the road were in the process of opening their shops for the day. Mendel tipped his felt hat to fellow businessmen pushing brooms on the sidewalk.

"John, you can hardly stay on that thing!" Roseweiz shouted out from under a light green awning. He owned a jewelry store one block away from the Mendel shop.

Herr Mendel responded by taking both hands off the handle bars and playing with his mustache. Such banter was typical of the Jewish shop owners on Leipziger Street.

Roseweiz waved him off, shaking his head. Mendel was well liked in the area for his honesty and gentleness, so the other shop owners were concerned about his injuries. Anna had helped her mother find room for all the food the neighbors had brought when visiting her father, many he had assisted in hard times.

The bright red lettering on the front glass of the *John J. Mendel Pawn Shop* appeared in the distance. Across the street the Kluger family belongings were stacked up in front of the bakery they lived over. Mendel got off the bike and walked it over to where Frank Kluger stood stuffing items into the trunk of his car. The Klugers owned one of the few cars in the city.

"Frank, what is going on? Are you leaving?" John asked, even though the answer was clear.

Kluger took a box from his young son and pushed it down hard into a tight space in the trunk. His thick brown mustache draped low over the corners of his mouth, so that one could barely see his lips move. "Ja, we are getting out while we still can and so should you!"

Mendel glanced as his daughter whose expression read, *I told you so.* "But this is your home, Frank. You're letting them drive you out. I have no intention moving anywhere. I am a German citizen!"

Kluger's eyes flared as he threw his hat down onto some luggage. "Your stubbornness will get you nothing! Do you not understand that? The Nazis will not be impressed by some prideful Jew?"

"The Nazis won't be around long, that type never is and some other party will take over." Mendel shrugged his shoulders.

Picking up his hat, Frank softened his tone. "They just beat the hell out of you. The next time you won't be so lucky."

"I try to tell him that this time is different, but my parents won't listen to me." Anna was pleased to find backing for her intuition.

Before John could reply Frank added, "Think of your family, if not for yourself." He looked at Anna. "Don't make them pay for your pride."

"We've been in Germany for centuries; I know that we should not have to leave here." She placed a hand on her father's arm, though she would have liked to throw her own suitcase into the trunk of that car.

John hopped back on his bike and bid Kluger a determined goodbye. "I'll see you after school!" He shouted to Anna.

It was not just a matter of pride that kept the Mendels from emigrating, but the taxes that had to be paid for an exit visa. They would have to sell everything they owned and then only be allowed to take 10 marks out of the country. The Nazi made it very difficult for Jews to leave Germany, while all the while complaining of their presence.

Anna watched as her father pedaled on to the shop. The Mendel family would never leave Germany voluntarily and the Nazis would not budge either. What kind of heinous retribution would there be for those Jews not willing or able to run? Already most in Germany hailed Hitler and his Brown Shirts. He was the new saint who was here to rescue Germany from the vermin infestations.

Two blocks away Ingrid stood waiting for Anna on the corner, rocking on her heels looking cheerful as always. Her friend appeared to be a in a foul mood again. Anna could look so old, if only she could approach life with a more light-hearted attitude. The waltz music coming from a nearby café contrasted with the glum expression of the dark haired

"Anna, come on! Smile, I promise it won't kill you. It might hurt just a little though." Ingrid joked

and pretended to conduct the orchestra. Life was becoming so complicated, so serious. She wanted to laugh, damn it!

As Anna got closer a sly grin emerged. "Okay, I'm smiling. You satisfied?" Anna asked cynically.

Ingrid inspected her friend coolly with tongue in check. "No, actually I'm not." She held her own school books out in front of her and dropped them to the ground. The loud thump echoed in the nearby alley and then Ingrid took Anna's and dropped them as well.

Anna was about to mouth a protest when she was whisked down the narrow alley in a waltz step. "Ingrid are you crazy?"

She stared up at the tall blonde who only raised an eyebrow in response. "What the hell are you doing?" Ingrid's grip was strong and her gray eyes commanded attention, they were such beautiful eyes.

Time seemed to vanish, along with the world as the two girls danced to music fading away in the distance. Anna's heart raced as Ingrid pulled her closer, until she could hear nothing but blood pounding in her ears and humming. Yes, Ingrid was humming! Anna slipped her arms around her friend to hang on.

They danced slower as the sunlight dimmed in the alley and Ingrid began to tire. All of a sudden Ingrid stopped moving and hugged Anna tight. It was as if they were both in trances and in some other plane of existence. Ingrid took Anna's face in her hands and turned it upward.

Anna thought that her heart must surely be a puddle between them as she studied the other girl's face in the soft light. Ingrid needed no make up to be beautiful. Then Ingrid pressed her red lips against Anna's and kissed her for the longest time. For a few moments they existed as one person and Anna did not care who might catch them. She had loved Ingrid since they were small children, but until that instant Anna had not realized that she was in love with her.

Ingrid stepped back looking stressed and confused. She swallowed hard and blinked rapidly."We're going to be late." She avoided the soft brown eyes of her friend and spoke in mumbled tones. *Did she really do that?* Still not making eye contact Ingrid turned and walked briskly down the alley to retrieve her books. She felt strange, warm all over, it was wrong, but Ingrid wanted to run back down that alley and kiss Anna again. *Why the hell didn't boys make her feel that way?*

Anna was stunned and happy as she watched Ingrid wave and then disappear down the street. What a feeling! Suddenly the problems all around her distant and she could not wait until that afternoon to see Ingrid again.

But Ingrid did not come to the shop or call. Days passed and Anna knew that Ingrid did not accept her feelings and was chastising herself for kissing another girl. Not just a girl, but a Jewish girl. If Anna could just talk with Ingrid she could make her see that everything was fine, nothing had to change. Was Ingrid scared or disgusted by her own feelings?

On the third day that Ingrid did not appear on the corner Anna let her tears fall with the cold, icy rain drops. The thought that one kiss could ruin their friendship made Anna's heart ache with regret and fear. Some people react violently to the parts of their hearts that they find embarrassing or offensive and will hurt others trying to cut that part out. What would Ingrid do, how far would she go?

Four

2006

Colorado

Anna Mendel rocked gently on her porch swing, waving at the children riding by on their bikes. She had delivered most of them as well as their parents in the sleepy little town of Wild-springs, Colorado. She had immigrated to the United States after the war, attended medical school at the University of Kansas and then settled down in the Rocky Mountains as they reminded her of Germany.

Not the Germany marred by the Nazis, but the one she remembered before the onslaught of hatred and uniformed thugs. She missed the beauty of Bavaria and happy German drinking songs, wonderful synagogues and churches standing strong against a bright blue sky.

At eighty-five Anna had lived a full life, even if not always a happy one. In Germany she had been persecuted for being a Jew, in America she had to hide most of her personal life to have a successful career. Only now in her autumn years did gay people finally have some source of security and in other countries were getting legally married.

She knew that most everyone in Wildsprings knew that Dr. Mendel and her roommate were more than friends, but no one bothered them over it. They were lucky to find such a peaceful, lovely town to make a life. It did not hurt that Anna had been the only doctor and Agnes Eichel the only veterinarian in the area either.

Agnes or Aggie as people knew her had been diagnosed with cancer ten years earlier and died shortly after. Losing her partner after forty years was traumatic for Anna and for the town folk who were reluctant to find another vet for their horses and pets. She was also a concentration camp survivor like Anna, for political crimes against the Nazi state at age fifteen.

Anna still lived in their two story house on the edge of town, the building where Agnes had her practice locked up and left untouched since her death. She had kept working up until she could no longer get out of bed. It was quiet now with no sounds of Aggie singing or whistling about the place.

It was a cloudy day with the leaves rustling gently in the cool breeze. The smell of pine and a scent of rain made Anna smile as she sat on her wraparound porch, sipping lemonade and reading the Denver Sunday paper.

She enjoyed retirement from her busy medical practice, though Anna had not hung up the stethoscope until age eighty-five at the same time as Agnes since they had plans to travel the world and return to Germany together. Cancer had put a stop to that adventure and Anna had no desire to visit her homeland alone.

The jovial morning mood was tainted by the article on the first page of the Denver Times as Anna flipped the paper out with both hands. Another former Nazi was being arrested by the Department of Justice under the Office of Special Operations. It was a woman who had been a camp guard at Ravensbrück and Auschwitz, but there was a twist to this story as the woman was Jewish and married to a rabbi. Well, this is different she thought.

Ingrid Goldsmith covered her face for the cameras as she was escorted from an award ceremony by federal agents. She would be tried for filing false information and concealing information on her citizenship application in 1949 rather than being immediately deported back to Germany.

On the application Goldsmith had claimed to be a concentration camp victim and she still maintained that assertion. It was contested by two witnesses, one a camp survivor who suffered at Levy's hands when she was known as Aufseherin Ingrid Brecht.

Nearly choking on her lemonade, Anna dropped the glass, which shattered all over the wooden porch painted a light gray. *Oh my God.* Her heart slammed against her sternum. She had not seen or heard about her childhood friend since January 1945 when Anna was released from Auschwitz at the orders of Oberaufseherin Brecht.

It was not a welcome memory. Mendel had fought hard to push the horror of Nazi Germany into the recesses of her brain and Anna had no desire to relive the past. Nothing was simple about that era, nothing black and white like the courts were now trying to lump it all. She had not known that Ingrid was a Nazi or camp guard until one fateful night in the Auschwitz infirmary, Christmas 1944.

Five

1942

Berlin

Ingrid had tossed and turned all that night after the waltz and kiss in the alley four years earlier. What had gotten into her? A simple dance to cheer Anna up was her only intention, but there was something about holding Anna close that released some courage that she did not know she possessed. Such boldness!

The dreams of that night nearly four years ago haunted her sleep with the softness of Anna's hair and the warmth of her skin taking Ingrid taking back in time. Anna was so much smaller, and frail, that protecting her made Ingrid feel like she could be good at something.

She would always regret not meeting Anna in the week after that dance since everything in Berlin started to turn bad for the Jews that April with the boycott of Jewish businesses. After that there was the burning of the synagogues and the breaking of all that storefront glass that the newspapers later called, "Kristallnacht."

Once free of Anna's influence though, Ingrid could appreciate the Nazi ideals and their hopes for Germany. She was getting along with her stepfather, Ernst, much better since Ingrid now wanted to hear about the discussions he had at the taverns.

In truth, Ingrid now sought any excuse to find fault with Anna and the Jews. It was much easier to endure the destruction of friends and neighbors when you no longer cared for them, when being patriotic dictated that for Germany's sake her true citizens had to make difficult choices. Sacrifices had to be made so that the most valuable Germans could survive

Most of the men were unemployed, thanks to certain elements encouraged by the Weimer Republic, which slowly eroded Germany with its leftish views. Ernst told Ingrid that it was that regime that had taken German women away from their roles as wives and mothers, sending them to universities to be doctors and the like!

Hitler was fixing Germany's issues and the unemployment rate with Jews now unable to practice medicine or law (as well as most women) nor could they practice pharmacology. The Nazis were also helping the unemployment rate by prohibiting the "double earners" of two income households with the wife naturally giving up her career.

Both Ingrid and her mother were members of the Frauenschaft (NSF), the Nazis women's group that encouraged the doctrine of the four Ks; Kinder, Kleider, Kirche and Kuche (Children, Clothes, Church and Kitchen). The philosophies of the Weimer era had made women like Gretchen Brecht feel inferior or even stupid for being content as wives and mothers.

Ingrid enjoyed being in the League of German Girls (BDM), which included vigorous physical exercise as well as ingraining the same ideals as the three Ks. It did occasionally occur to Ingrid that the Mendels, for the most part, also believed the same way. Anna's mother and sister both saw their roles as wives and mothers as their "careers" in life and took them very seriously. Only Anna had wanted more and was devastated when the university students had backed the Nazis and initiated book burning.

It was necessary for Ingrid to find fault with the girl she had loved and trusted for years. Many times she had watched Anna from a distance since that fateful day, but with her new BDM and Hitler Youth friends it was not possible to be best friends with a Jew. Ingrid had to convince herself that Anna was not good for her and associating with Jews would only hurt her family. There was no turning back at this point.

Sometimes Ingrid would stand across the street and stare at the Mendel shop with its busted windows and anti-Semitic graffiti painted all over the brick front. She would join in with her new friends as they paid tribute to Hitler, but deep down she wanted to run over to the Mendel apartment and stay there in the warm, kindly atmosphere where Frau Mendel was always baking bread.

Well, that was part of the past now. Ingrid had been scheduled to spend her Pflichjahr (Duty Year) at a farm doing manual labor, but fate intervened when Ingrid went to the tavern to fetch Ernst Brecht for supper.

It was a chore she hated as all the men made some remark about her looks, but this time a Major Richstatter of the Waffen

THE GOOD NAZI | 47

SS was sitting at her stepfather's table. It was sort of a mutual admiration moment as the two people studied each other.

Richstatter was about forty, with black hair that was gray at the temples. His blues eyes and tanned skin from serving in Africa were striking against his black uniform. When he smiled at her, his pink lips spread to reveal perfect, white teeth.

Ernst introduced her with his usual pride, which made her feel like a thoroughbred horse since the source of his sudden respect centered on her ability to breed Aryan children for Germany. He went on to explain that Ingrid would be leaving for agricultural duty in the east.

Shaking his head, Richstatter pulled a chair out for her to sit next to him. He asked if farm work was something she wanted to do. Ernst warned her with his expression to lie, but Ingrid had the feeling that she should be honest with this officer.

Before she could reply, however, the major bent over and pulled out colorful propaganda posters from a leather briefcase. He explained that the women in the poster were real Aryan women that were used for models. Ingrid was much prettier and would look extraordinary in an SS Lagen- fuhrerin (camp leader) uniform.

The Waffin SS was recruiting young women to work as camp guards throughout Germany and Richstatter wanted Ingrid to be a model for those posters. If Ingrid could help her country find the best recruits, then perhaps the SS could find a factory security job for Ernst? She felt her face heat up. There was no choice here really. Who would say no to an SS officer? Ingrid would also be denying her stepfather a job, which would lead to her mother being knocked around.

Ernst had accepted the offer before Ingrid could say a word. In an instant the Brecht financial woes were cured and all she would have to do is sit on a stool and look beautiful for posters to be printed by *R. Barnick GmbH*, the same company that Ernst would guard at night.

That conversation took place two months ago and while her stepfather was pleased, Ingrid was bored and did not feel very useful, no matter what pep talks Richstatter and her parents gave her.

Sitting in one place motionless for thirty minutes at a time was harder than shoveling snow.

The artists were mostly foreign laborers with the present one being from France. He was a slight, nervous man who seemed to be terrified of Ingrid, who made no attempt to keep her irritation a secret. Most of the artists worked quickly, but Frog, as she called him, kept making mistakes and had to paint over her face.

Ingrid arrived at work then went to change into the Lager-fuhrerin uniform in the small costume room. It was similar to a SS officer's, but hers came with a skirt and cape that added an almost vampire quality to the ensemble. Standing before a full length mirror, Ingrid had to admit that the black uniform gave her a majestic appearance.

When she entered the studio, the Frenchman, whose name was really Jean Gagne, bowed politely to the woman he called, the *Ice Maiden*. Frauline Brecht was beautiful but no matter how hard he tried, Jean could not capture the woman's features. If today was not successful he would be shipped back to Sachen-hausen.

Technical issues were not causing the problem, as her features were well defined with strong angles; he was letting his emotions get in the way. She scared the hell out of him.

Ingrid glided across the cluttered room to perch on the stool where she had already spent five hours the day before. She slipped into the pose as if someone had suddenly poured ice water over her, but those gray eyes watched his every move, every expression that might tell her how the work was going.

The artist painted remarkably slowly and the model sitting in the hot uniform cast a mean expression as time wore on. The displeasure showed in a darkening of her eyes. Jean bid her to relax for a moment while he assessed his progress.

Ingrid slid off the stool to stretch stiff and aching muscles. She watched gravely as the man shook his head at the canvas and felt a rage coming on. *Why was this clown still not satisfied?*

"Frauline, please excuse me, but you are changing your facial expressions just a bit and I cannot capture a true likeness." Jean illustrated his point with a downward motion of his brush.

"Seven hours and you still do not have it right? We've wasted all this time?" The statuesque blonde stormed off the platform where the stool was placed against a white background.

"I am so sorry, but you have a very special face that demands perfection. We'll start again tomorrow, yes?" Jean knew that he was close to suffering dire consequences for his failure.

"Oh no, damn it. Since you have perfection to work with, why should I pay for your lack of skill?" Ingrid's voice rose harshly. "Maybe you're not worth a shit as a painter and can't live up to your task." Ingrid's voice carried a cold, cutting quality that hurt more than her words.

Jean hated working with this conceited giant of a woman. She totally lacked sensitivity, though she possessed an unearthly gracefulness for such a large person. He would have to pacify her somehow since the Nazis had no shortage of painters. "We have orders to produce a magnificent work that will make every young woman in the Reich want to be like you. One more day, please Madame. I promise it will be the last. I know it's my fault and not to make excuses, but I've never had a subject so beautiful and it is overwhelming."

Ingrid watched as the painter's shoulders dropped in submission. "Okay, Frog, but tomorrow we *will* make a wonderful poster." It was not a suggestion and her tone indicated as such.

Jean bowed slightly as she left the room knowing that his days outside a concentration camp were nearly over.

She changed quickly then left the building. Ingrid closed her eyes and took a deep breath as she stepped outside. Two months she had been at this "sitting" business and was becoming more impatient as the days wore on. She was tired of staring at the same little man day after day. He was a Jew plucked from one of the camps for his talent in portraits, but Ingrid had failed to notice any such ability.

The posters bearing her noble face were all over Germany, earning her the awe of former classmates. They also commanded respect from strangers who assumed that Ingrid must be a real Lagerfuhrerin, a Schutzstaffel (SS) auxiliary with unknown powers. The combination of her looks and the uniform design scared everyone around her and Ingrid was beginning to enjoy it.

When she arrived home Ernst made a fuss over her since Ingrid was his pride and joy now. Next to downing a mug of brew, he most liked to brag about his stepdaughter and the future that had opened up to her.

Ingrid smirked; the drunken slob nearly had an orgasm at the mere mention of the SS. She was performing a valuable service, so that somehow gave him the license to become completely worthless. Ernst had called in sick numerous times since starting his factory job, but with Ingrid's earnings it was not necessary for him to work very hard. He might be a fool, but if he took his stepdaughter for one he was very mistaken.

"So, how is our little Nazi?" Brecht asked as he slurped beer on the couch. He had worked the nightshift and was still wearing uniform pants with a dirty undershirt. "Ready to conquer the world yet?" He belched the last few words.

"Give me time. I've not won over Berlin yet." She tossed her cap onto a chair. "One more day with Frog and I'll kill him. He better get it right tomorrow!"

Her stepfather downed the last of the beer, titling his head all the way back to get every drop. "What can you expect? The French spend all their time drinking wine and having orgies."

She slipped off her shoes and sat at the opposite end of the couch. "The little worm wants to start all over again, shit."

"HE decided to start all over? That scum can't tell you how it will be. Stand up to that little prick!" Ernst wiped the beer from his mouth with the back of a hairy hand.

Ingrid was silent for a moment. It had not occurred to her to stand up to him, to any man for that matter. The New Order required women to be submissive to men, but perhaps it did not mean all men. "You're right. If he doesn't finish that poster tomorrow morning I'm through with him." She coughed lightly. "He's just some half-assed Jew painter.

"That's our girl." Ernst replied with her mother sitting on the couch arm next to him. Gretchen beamed because the creep was finally working. Ingrid's parents made her sick with her step-father being an asshole and her mother taking it. Women were supposed to save Germany by saving the German family, which meant being subservient and having babies for Hitler. There did not seem to be a solution for worthless German men.

"I'm going to change before supper." Ingrid grabbed her cap and went to her room.

She had moved the furniture around since Anna was there last and burned any reminder of her friend in a ceremony while her stepfather looked on. That little party really pleased Ernst and convinced him that she had truly reformed. What he did not know was that Ingrid kept a small photograph of Anna hidden in her jacket pocket. Anna had been gone long enough that she seemed vague, like a dream that lingers long after waking.

In some ways Ingrid did not want to remember the past as for all her good qualities, Anna was still a Jew. She worked for the S.S. now and was beginning to understand the Jewish problem. Still something kept her from throwing the last picture away. A pounding headache prompted Ingrid to turn in early.

The night was long and restless with dreams of that twit of an artist never finishing the poster. She woke in a bad mood and arrived at the studio void of patience. He was too damned picky with some oddball notion of perfection.

Jean was prepping his brushes and palette and had already stretched a new canvas when Ingrid stepped up on the stage. He smiled. "Ready to start?" Jean asked her in a soft, pleasant voice. *Must not anger the Goddess!* If he were to ever desire to die in a camp all he need do is tell her what a pompous, evil, unbearable ass she was, but then he probably would not make it that far. She would gut him right then and there and hang his innards from the ceiling.

"I see that you are starting all over again? Was that really necessary?" Ingrid asked in a threatening tone.

"I'm sure that all we need is a fresh start. We'll be done soon." What little optimism he had faded quickly.

Jean painted quickly for an hour, ever watching the expression of his model. It was not going well and he suggested that she take a break. He was not going to capture whatever it was that made her Ingrid Brecht. She had an unusually elegant, noble look that she wore most of the time. There was something elusive in her eyes, in the shape of her mouth that just escaped the paint soaked bristles of his brush. Ingrid had a fearful mix of beauty and cruelty that eluded reproduction. What attracted people to her could not be copied.

When she returned from break Ingrid had two Nazi officers with her. She went back to the stool and struck her usual pose while the two men took a seat near Jean. *Why were they here?* He felt his heart pound hard, knocking against his sternum. Working with them watching was like doing a command performance for Satan. One of them was Richstatter, but Jean did not know the other one of a higher rank.

"Jean, don't let us bother you. Please continue." Richstatter smiled, crossing his legs, the jackboots gleaming under the lights. The Nazis certainly believed in pomp.

Ingrid sat poised, retaining her icy expression. She had run into her two superiors outside. The one called Zimmerman was there to observe the art studio. She was not sure why as he was a battlefield officer not involved with propaganda, but the real thing. He was really serving the Reich, not sitting on a hard stool and Ingrid envied him.

The artist acted strangely, peering up at her often. Usually he glanced at her sparingly, staring intently at the canvas. Maybe he was closed to finishing?

The Frenchman was sweating, he felt as if he had a high fever. The harder he tried the further away from Ingrid's likeness he went. He was both furious with himself and horrified of her reaction upon discovering his failure. Fortunately, the two officers seemed more interested in Ingrid than him, but it did not cease his growing fear. The picture was a flop. He could not keep working on it any longer. She would find out sooner or later.

Jean was cleaning his brushes! Suddenly Ingrid relaxed, grinned at nothing in particular and stretched her long legs. She waited for the painter to say something, her mood hanging in the balance as she analyzed his behavior.

Colonel Zimmerman clung to Ingrid Brecht's every move, carefully noting her reaction to the situation. This girl was more than model material. In fact, she was too hard boiled even for the Gestapo; the S.S. could use a woman like her. At the moment she smiled sweetly and was very pretty, but a short while ago she wore a mask that could have been cast in hell. He squinted curiously at the artist who just suddenly dropped his arms to his side. The painter never took his eyes off his subject.

The painter and the model locked stares for a moment then the Frenchman shook his head very slowly from side to side. The happiness in Ingrid's face crawled from her features in such a manner that it reminded him of a phonograph record being played at too slow a speed. She rose to her full height and leaped off the stage. Ingrid snatched the canvas from the easel and studied the figure on it. Her head titled slightly and a sneer crossed her face as she slung the painting into the far wall. The gray eyes seemed to frost over as Ingrid slammed the heavy easel into Jean. Before he could run she retrieved the stool and broke it over his head.

As Jean tried to crawl out from under the easel, she poured turpentine over his broken nose. Blood ran from his nose and mingled with the paint lobbed on his shirt. The victor stood over him breathing heavy, a calmness weaving its way back into her expression. She looked at the two observers with no sign of regret or apology.

"Mueller! Come get this man and take him to the hospital, then have someone clean up this mess." Richstatter was notably taken back at the episode. He seemed to want to say something to Zimmerman but could not find the words. He feared the consequences of Fraulein Brecht's actions.

Zimmerman pondered the wild girl for a moment, nodding his head. Ingrid would be excellent working as a camp guard, not just recruiting them. The future plan of the Third Reich called for good Aryans able to carry out difficult, but necessary tasks for Germany. With the jails filling up with more criminals, especially females, camps were being built to house them. There was a training facility for guards at Ravensbrück north of Berlin.

"Ingrid, would you like to join the S.S. Auxiliary as a camp guard and actually one day get to wear that Lagerfuhrerin uniform?" Zimmerman asked somberly, ignoring the amazed look on Richstatter's face.

She studied him for a moment as if just awakening from a nap. "Yes sir, I would very much like the opportunity."

"Very good. Why don't you go freshen up while I discuss it with Major Richstatter." Zimmerman framed the order as a suggestion.

When the irate model had left the room the Major stood up. "Are you serious? After such a display it's clear to me that she will be hard to control."

Zimmerman eased out of his chair and walked around the cluttered room. "I see something else, Major. Passion and ambition are traits I can work with and, as you know, it takes a certain type of woman to maintain order in the camps."

"Yes, of course you know best. When would you like her to report?" Richstatter suddenly felt relieved that Brecht was leaving. His military career centered on journalism and regimental histories, not brutality. Suddenly Ingrid's cool charm had turned sour for him.

When she returned Ingrid appeared calm, watching impassively as low ranking SS men cleaned up the mess. She remembered attacking Jean, but the act meant little to her and Ingrid made no apology for it.

"Ingrid, report to my office tomorrow morning and we'll start the application process for the SS Helferinnenkorps (Corps of SS Assistants). You'll have to meet the same qualifications as the men, but I don't see that as a problem." Zimmerman smiled at the woman who was slightly taller.

Ingrid looked to Richstatter for approval since he had, after all, kept her from digging in the dirt on some wretched farm. He nodded. "Yes sir!" The gleam on her face made her even more beautiful.

"Congratulations Ingrid, I know you will do well and I hope you find some of the excitement you desire. You were a wonderful model though, and perhaps this will encourage even more young women to join us." Richstatter offered his hand.

"You will be trained at FKL Ravensbrück, a beautiful area that I'm sure you will enjoy. Be at my office at 8am and we'll get you started on your way." Zimmerman patted her on the shoulder.

Six

1938-1944

Germany

A few months after Anna danced with Ingrid, the Nazis orchestrated reprisals against the Jews by having SA members destroy shops and synagogues while wearing civilian clothes. It was done to convince the world that the German people had had enough of conniving, greedy Jews. The uprising was dubbed by the media as, *The Night of the Broken Glass.*

John Mendel had heard of the commotion that night in November from a neighbor and hurried to his store to find all the windows shattered. The glass shards had sparkled in red and gold hues from the flames of the bookstore across the street. What the thieves did not want they threw in a pile outside the store near books burning for the good of the Reich.

Without his knowledge, Anna had followed her father and was outraged at the sight. One of the thugs draped a sign that read, *Jude*, over John Mendel's head and gave him a bugle to play. She recognized one of them as Heinz Gruber, the Brown

Shirt that had harassed them before. He laughed while mocking her father and then Gruber kicked Mendel hard in the back. In a fury, Anna had grabbed a heavy book and pitched it at Gruber's face. It broke his nose and injured his left eye.

The policemen instructed to ignore the vandalism by the Nazis had no trouble arresting Anna Mendel for battery. When booked into jail, she was beaten for her attitude then thrown into an overcrowded cell with murderers, thieves, prostitutes and other women victimized for being born Jews.

After a year in that hellhole Anna was transferred to a farm to grow produce for the Fatherland. She was not used to hard labor or the long hours and suffered terribly before physically and mentally adjusting to the change. The matrons supervising were vicious bitches who thoroughly enjoyed their lot in life, but it was good to be outside in the fresh air and sunshine after the dank, stinking confines of the city jail. The old couple, who had originally owned the farm before the Nazis stole it were gentle people who clearly did not approve of the rough treatment.

From the start it was clear that Anna's intellect was superior to most of the other "criminals" doing time for the Reich. She was organized, observant, logical and spotted bookkeeping errors just from glancing at the spreadsheets while sweeping the office. It was not long before Anna's full time job was doing the books and ordering supplies, which put her in contact with Dirk Morgenstern.

Morgenstern was a strapping, gregarious man well liked and fully trusted by the Nazis overseeing the farm. He sold seed and purchased produce for his small store in the nearby village of Holtzstadt in Bavaria.

The population of Holtzstadt was 456 with few of the inhabitants thrilled over Hitler's government. Many of the village youth had refused to join the Hitler youth group and instead had formed a band fashioned after the Cologne group, The Edelweiss Pirates. While not quite as aggressive or inventive as the larger group, the Mountain Pirates served the cause by aiding those escaping from the labor camps, and at times organizing those escapes.

Dirk had a niece and nephew working in his store that were members of the Mountain Pirates. Miles and Hannah Berge took a liking to Anna early on, slipping her extra rations and bringing news from the outside that she shared with other inmates.

Two months after Anna arrived at the farm she escaped with the groups' help and a year with them sabotaging supply trains, stealing food, hiding Jews and aiding in the escape of others from various labor camps. In November 1943 Anna Mendel was captured by Nazi soldiers when a bridge the Pirates tried to blow up failed to collapse. The charge was placed in the wrong spot, which allowed the troop transport to cross the bridge where the group watched the ordeal from the woods.

She was soon on a passenger train to Ravensbrück, a camp for women criminals and enemies of the Reich north of Berlin. In a way, Anna was lucky that the officer in charge was a career military man and thought the youthful Anna should be arrested and not executed on site, like two of the Pirate men.

Ravensbrück was far worse than the farm labor camp and the guards there made the labor camp guards appear as milk maids in comparison. Newly recruited guards were schooled at Ravensbrück in a three week training period. Anna had no way of knowing it, but her friend, Ingrid Brecht had gone through the training and was transferred to Auschwitz just six months earlier.

The camp was arranged in blocks overseen by guards not only encouraged to be vicious, but punished for not being so, as Anna had seen happen when the occasional Aufseherin would show kindness instead of brutality. They had assistants taken from the criminal inmates called Kapos who were just as mean and controlling as their Nazi supervisors.

Anna had heard that the camp was once clean when there were only 250 women per building, but the numbers had grown to the point that four and five times that amount were cramped into each block. She shared a bed with three other women and there were some people who slept on the floor with no blankets. Stealing was rampant, demanding that anything of value had to be stuffed into the pockets of rough striped dresses worn twenty-four hours a day, seven days a week.

Anna worked for several weeks on a road crew clearing fallen trees and branches off the roads during a winter storm when she first encountered the guards with dogs. The German Shepherds were used to discourage prisoners from running off into the woods, but some of the Aufseherin would command the dogs to attack the poor, sick, stick thin women for no reason at all. It made her so angry that she could no nothing about it without great personal harm.

One of the guards who liked to use her dog as a weapon was called Grese. Most of the time the inmates never learned a guard's name, but this one was different for both her cruelty and her incredible beauty. It was a strange twist of logic for such a pretty face to harbor such an ugly soul. After the war Anna learned that Irma Grese had been tried for war crimes and hung and she was glad for it. However, there were many more who wandered out of the camps and off the radar to live out normal lives.

Life was miserable and women did nearly anything to improve their lots in the camp. Ravensbrück was a main pool from which the SS brothels were stocked. Some prisoners believed that volunteering would lead to better treatment and more rations than the wretched life in the main camp and on the labor crews. The truth was that most died very quickly from venereal disease or sadistic sexual abuse by SS personnel.

Sex was something the Nazis appeared to value, especially between male SS staff and their auxiliaries, the Aufseherin. Breeding for the Fuhrer! A few of the Aufseherin had sexual relationships with both Nazi male lovers and female inmates. Grese was one such guard. Anna was grateful that the she-devil never noticed her.

One of the camp doctors recognized Anna and told the SS Major he worked under that she was very intelligent and would make a good worker at the electronics plant, Seimens, which used slave labor from Ravensbrück to manufacture their products. It was at Seimens that Anna Mendel bought her ticket to Auschwitz and her fateful rendezvous with Ingrid Brecht.

Seven

2006

Kansas

The Federal judge determined that Mrs. Levy was not a flight risk nor a risk to herself or other people, much to the chagrin of the woman who reported her, Katrinia Schiffer, and thus went home the next morning unlike the many prisoners at Auschwitz over sixty years earlier.

Ingrid had no memory of the angry woman who wanted her deported to Germany. She was a Polish Jew who had married a German man and for that crime he had died at Sachenhausen near Berlin and Ravensbrück. There was nothing more disgusting to the Nazis than being a race traitor.

Mrs. Schiffer had never remarried and was not a religious Jew, but did come for the High Holy Day services to hear the new rabbi, Levy. She had not seen that Aufseherin since 1944, but such a face she could not forget or the cruelty of the woman wearing it. The rabbi's wife was a Nazi.

The venom in Schiffer's eyes and her voice was shocking to Ingrid and embarrassing as she had watched the faces of her husband and her many flabbergasted friends since her arrest. At first everyone was certain the woman was mistaken. Ingrid was a camp survivor herself and a champion of the Jewish community since her arrival in the United States in 1948. How could she have ever been a Nazi camp guard?

Ingrid's only statement to the media had been that she was indeed a former Auschwitz inmate and had suffered terribly there. The attorney hired by her husband told her to say nothing else until he had a chance to speak with her further. Michael Eisen had ancestors who died in the camps; grandparents, aunts, uncles and cousins that he never got to meet. Since he was a member of Temple Beth-El, Eisen took her case without hesitation.

The initial appointment Eisen made with Ingrid he made with her alone. He wanted the whole story, guts and all and she was not likely to be as frank with her rabbi husband in the room. His office overlooked a large pond in Wichita on grounds that used to be owned by Beech Aircraft for its employees enjoyment. Michael remembered picnicking and fishing there was a boy when his father worked for Olive Beech, a well liked business woman in the area.

He continued looking over the basic information he had on the case, which was spread out over a large, maple desk, while occasionally glancing at the deep blue water of the pond covered with gentle waves. The view was costly, but worth it.

It was unfathomable to Eisen that Ingrid was lying and yet, it was also hard to believe that Schiffer could be so completely wrong. It had been sixty-two years since Katrinia Schiffer had allegedly seen Ingrid beating people at Ravensbrück, how could she have such a good memory after all that time? It had been forty-five years since a neighborhood bully had pounded the hell out of Eisen, but he could remember every freckle on the punk's face and the smell of his cheap Christmas stocking cologne. Never underestimate the power of anger and humiliation in memory recall.

Ingrid Levy arrived for her afternoon appointment fifteen minutes early. The woman who prior to the accusations had always been smiling and pleasant was now drawn and ash colored with her eyes full of sadness. He had his secretary bring her some water and coffee.

Even at eighty-five, Ingrid Levy was elegant and appeared twenty years younger. Her tall, trim frame settled gracefully into the armchair across from the lawyer's desk. He allowed her to take several sips of coffee before jumping in.

"Let's start off with a question. Is there any truth to what Schiffer is saying?" Eisen leaned back in his chair.

Ingrid placed the cup and saucer on his desk. "Yes" She watched for his reaction, but could see nothing obvious.

He leaned back and placed his elbows on the desk. "Okay, how did a guard end up with a concentration camp number on her arm?"

"Because I did the unforgiveable-I was kind to someone and had her released from Auschwitz. I never expected to live through it honestly." A great burden seemed to lift from her shoulders and they immediately sagged.

"You took a great risk to save someone? Who?" Eisen readied his pen for a name.

"A childhood friend, my best friend, Anna Mendel. I found her in the infirmary, nearly dead. An SS officer I was involved with, Heinz Gruber, noticed Anna was there and told me. We all went to the same secondary school once, what you call high school. By that time Hans was as fed up as me with the whole mess." The events were so long ago that Ingrid felt like she was describing a movie.

"So was Anna released then?" Eisen asked.

"Yes, around Christmas, before the death marches started. I escaped in January, 1945 when the camp was being evacuated before the Russians could get there. Some of the guards were sympathetic to me and looked the other way when I bolted for the forest." Ingrid folded her arms tightly as if back in the frigid Polish woods. The Russians found me when I backtracked to the camp and sought shelter."

"What happened to Anna?" Eisen hoped the woman had survived.

"I don't know. I never saw her again." Tears welled up in Ingrid's eyes.

"I appreciate the risk you took to save Anna, but we have a problem Ingrid. You entered the country under the Displaced Persons Act of 1948 and the INS will state that you misrepresented yourself. The Holtzman Amendment of 1978 orders the deportation of those who ordered, incited, assisted, or participated in persecution in connection with the German Nazi regime." Eisen paused.

"But I have spent fifty years being a good person! I have done nothing morally or criminally wrong since being in America." Ingrid's features grew animated.

"I know that, Ingrid, but anyone that participated in the Nazi regime as a guard is not eligible and is specifically excluded." Michael felt for the woman seated across from him who he could not picture in a Nazi uniform terrorizing people.

"What can I do then? This is my home...I don't know anybody in Germany anymore." Storm clouds seemed to cover her gray eyes.

"There will be a hearing and, of course I will put up a defense since you were also a prisoner and did in fact help another escape. Your conduct as a U.S. citizen for the past fifty years will be presented, but I need to know the complete truth about your service to the Third Reich. There are four witnesses who remember you from the camps. Two from Ravensbrück and one from Auschwitz. Their testimony is devastating." He paused as he read the file. "If in fact you were Ingrid Brecht."

"I was told there were only three witnesses." Ingrid appeared worried. "What do you mean if I was?"

"More have come forward since the press ran with the story. One made a statement about Ravensbrück, a Greta Hamlin, from the village of Furstenberg. Are you familiar with the town?" Eisen asked her.

"It was across the lake from the camp. What does she have to say about me? When I went to town it was certainly not with inmates." The rabbi's wife straightened up in her chair, a slight hint of superiority seeping through.

He tapped his finger on Hamlin's statement. "Well, she claims to have watched you on a road crew from the forest and she has some very unflattering things to say about your treatment of prisoners. Did you have a dog, Ingrid?" Eisen watched her reaction carefully.

Ingrid appeared dumbstruck. "Only for a short while before I was transferred to Auschwitz." Her throat tightened and her voice became froggy. "It was so very long ago, I was young and STUPID!" She spit the words out and tears fell.

"I know, I know, let's just take this one step at a time. What did you do with the dog?" The lawyer asked his voice low and calm.

She struggled to stop the tears by biting her lip. "I was cruel...very very cruel. I made the dog bite the women's legs and feet, he ripped gashes in their flesh and when they would try to run away, I would let go of his leash. Please, it was terrible. The dog mangled their already freezing limbs...is that what this Greta saw?" Ingrid inquired as she pulled a tissue from a box on Eisen's desk.

"Yes, she was keeping a diary that ran several months with eye witness accounts of you and your fellow guards. She was a member of the Nazi party, so little attention was paid to her actions. Greta was in fact also working for the resistance. She recognized your picture when it posted by a Holocaust survivors group in Florida. The other witness from Ravensbrück is a man, Herman Weiss, who worked in the infirmary. He witnessed poor treatment as he moved around the camp."

He studied the file for a moment. "Actually, I'm most concerned about two women from Auschwitz who were directly affected by your behavior as a guard. Do you recall anything about them? There is Katrina Schiffer and Ursela Mendehoff?"

Ingrid shook her head. "I'm ashamed to say it, but there were so many inmates that I don't recall very many personally."

"These women state that you enjoyed being abusive and you were a friend of Maria Mandel, a chief supervisor at Auschwitz. I did a little research on her and it does not look good, Ingrid. In fact, the witnesses say that Maria gave you a black uniform like hers and that you seemed to be best friends." Eisen hoped it was not true.

Mandel's reputation as a Nazi guard was notorious. She savored choosing women and children for the gas chamber and was executed in Poland for her crimes in 1948, the same year Ingrid left for the United States. Prisoners had called her, The Beast.

"I met her at Ravensbrück and yes, she was mean, but you have to understand that we had no choice. We were young, naive and if we did not perform as expected in the three week training course we could end up as inmates ourselves. I saw it happen! She remembered me from our training when I was transferred to Auschwitz and took me under her wing." Ingrid bristled somewhat at being judged and Eisen noticed.

"The hearing is in three months in Kansas City. I would like you to write down what you did at both camps and then I'd like a list of character witnesses to testify about the good character you have shown the past fifty years. Can you do that?" Eisen looked her in the eyes.

She nodded. "Yes, I think so."

"This is only the beginning Ingrid. People are going to be outraged and offended, even those who have known you the past five decades and worked alongside you. I need to know everything you did. I can't have any surprises in that courtroom from witnesses. The best defense here is to deny being Ingrid Brecht."

She swallowed hard, struggling to control her emotions. "I've spent years trying to bury that horror. I am truly not that Ingrid Brecht anymore."

Eisen pulled out copies of three old photographs. "I don't believe you are either and if Nazi records list you as the inmate Ingrid Goldstein it will be near impossible to refute it. Take these pictures and try to recall if these women have any special reason remember you."

Ingrid Levy gathered up the pictures and placed them in the dark green purse that matched her dress. "Thank you for taking my case. I know it's not the popular thing to do."

"I think the sophistication of a society is determined by the fairness of its laws and the unbiased application of those laws. I can't guarantee that you will not be deported or denaturalized, but I will do my best to defend you. Besides, even if you lose, I can appeal for years." He shrugged his shoulders.

Eight

2006

Kansas

That night Rabbi Levy had a heated argument with his wife of fifty-five years. It had been building since her arrest in front of all their friends and congregants. While he was second generation American, the Rabbi had relatives and many friends who had suffered at the hands of the Nazis in Europe. Herschel was humiliated publicly and betrayed and hurt personally by a woman that he thought he knew.

Photographs of Ingrid as a camp guard confronted him nearly daily as the media latched onto the story. Of course he could hardly blame journalists for grabbing headlines with such a situation as a rabbi married to a former Nazi. It was almost a joke.

To make matters worse, Ingrid responded must the same as other charged with war crimes. *It was a different time, we only followed orders, you don't understand,* and perhaps it was true. Levy was so angry that he was not sure his marriage could survive or that it should. He would never have been involved with Ingrid if he had known her past.

The past week Levy had tried to put on a good face for his congregation, to be the leader he was paid to be, but it was excruciating knowing what they were thinking. How could he not know? What kind of moron could be so ignorant?

He remembered the sweet, pretty German woman he met in 1950, so strong and passionate about supporting the Jewish tradition and a symbol of triumph over evil. The perfect wife for a rabbi and Ingrid Goldman would fill that role flawlessly for years.

As they shouted at each other Herschel saw a different look in her eyes or was he imagining it? It was a cold gleam he had not seen before and suddenly he found himself seeing her in a Nazi uniform ready to strike him down. Levy did not know how to feel about the woman who had slept next to him for over five decades.

He fully expected to be asked to resign as rabbi, that was a given. Why not? Was he not a collaborator of sorts helping to hide a war criminal in plain sight? Herschel was in the middle of a shout in response to Ingrid saying something about forgiveness when his heart seized.

As he fell to the floor the rabbi saw Ingrid rush to his side with the mobile phone calling 911. It seemed an eternity before the ambulance arrived to whisk him off to Wesley Medical Center. After that the rabbi knew nothing until he woke up in the surgical intensive care unit recovering from open heart surgery.

With a tube down his throat he could not speak, but was alert enough to know that there was tension between his wife and their children who had arrived from Illinois. David and

Sarah both had two children each who were the joy of their grandparent's lives. It had to be very hard on them too with the children in high school and college.

When Ingrid took his hand Herschel's eyes teared up. If only the past weeks had not happened. If only he did not know the truth about her. Who ever had said ignorance was bliss was right. She had changed from the woman she had been in Nazi Germany, but who had she really been then? Ingrid was barely eighteen when she volunteered for the guards, should that be considered?

Nothing would ever be the same regardless of the outcome of the hearing. If by some accident Ingrid was allowed to stay in the country Herschel would never look at his wife the same again and neither would their children. David and Sarah were still in a state of shock having a difficult time believing their mother was the stern appearing guard on the Nazi identification card in the news.

If Ingrid were deported the rabbi would not go with her to Germany. He had no life or family there. All his responsibilities were in America. Such worries were not good for a man just out of quadruple bypass surgery and a week after being discharged Rabbi Levy collapsed and died leaving his children and grandchildren with only Ingrid for support.

She sat down with David and Sarah and tried to explain why she had deceived them, but her words felt empty as they tumbled out of Ingrid's mouth. The children seemed to understand why she joined the guards as work was scarce and it was the best option at the time, what they did not understand was the amount of cruelty their mother was accused of inflicting on helpless inmates.

Ingrid feared the hearing and the testimony of those who knew her so many years ago during Hitler's reign of terror. She did not want her family there to hear it, but both children planned on being there despite their mother's protests.

The lawyer wanted names of people to bear witness to her good works and rehabilitation, but how could she call people and ask them to defend her? She had betrayed everyone who knew her, especially her own husband who now lay in a coffin partly due to the stress the whole mess placed on him. Ingrid knew of only one person to rely on.

Nine

1943

Ravensbrück, Germany

The training period at Ravensbrück was worse than Ingrid could ever have imagined. She was capable of losing her temper and being a tyrant as she had with the French painter, but the Nazis required that level of anger and disregard all the time. Even when she thought that her level of discipline was adequate she would be slapped or humiliated by one of the Aufseherin training them.

For three weeks she endured and hardened to the satisfaction of the camp supervisors, one of whom was Maria Mandel. Ingrid told her about Ernst Brecht and how it would be impossible to fail and return home. Maria helped Ingrid turn into a guard the SS was proud to claim. The new guard exceeded their expectations in the year before she would follow Mandel to Auschwitz.

Ravensbrück provided ample opportunities for an ambitious guard with no regard for hurt feelings or private property, not that the prisoners had much to steal. After awhile being superior was like an adrenaline rush. Power was addictive and the longer Ingrid wielded it the better she got at intimidating and terrorizing women into obeying her every command. She smiled slightly whenever she saw the sudden snaps to attention when prisoners knew she was coming.

The Third Reich would last one thousand years and Ingrid was part of it from the ground up. Germany had a wonderful destiny for those capable of leading the German people into the future and Ingrid Brecht was one of the chosen ones. It was a far cry from the wretched life she knew in Berlin where Ingrid had nothing to look forward to but her stepfather's drunken tirades. He did not dare mess with her now and it was a wonderful feeling for a young woman in Nazi Germany. If not for the camps, Ingrid had no future outside being a wife and mother for the Fuehrer.

Sometimes at night when Ingrid lay in bed unable to sleep she thought of Anna Mendel and momentarily would feel guilt and shame for her treatment of Jews and other inmates. Anna had kept Ingrid in balance, kept her from jumping into the abyss, but her friend also made Ingrid soft, too kind in a time where such traits got one fingered to the Gestapo. With the brutality and lack of compassion abounding having a heart easily broken was foolish, so she pushed memories of childhood out of sight and mind. It was the only way she could do her job successfully.

Maria Mandel recommended Ingrid Brecht for the work patrols when she indicated boredom with camp life. She thought Brecht would handle a dog well and keep prisoners at labor instead of running off. She was right. Nothing abated anger and frustration like a position of power where there were no limits or punishments for excessive force.

After a long day of working in the freezing cold Ingrid would retire to her warm cottage and several roommates where they would eat dinner before a roaring fire. She and her companions were volunteers for the SS auxiliary, meaning that they were an elite group that met the same strict qualifications as the SS men. There were Aufseherin who were conscripted into service, but such women were held in less regard having been forced to work for the Reich.

A few months after being assigned to the labor patrol Ingrid was reassigned to training new guards, a position she relished and where her sadism blossomed. There was no turning back to the old days when little Ingrid would share a delicious Sabbath meal with the Mendels then squeeze into bed with Anna and giggle until drifting off to sleep. The stuff of childhood was not a luxury servants of the New Order could afford.

At least that is the sort of thing she told herself when women cried and screamed at Ingrid's abuse and begged for food or blankets earning her laughter or a viscous kick in response. Occasionally a man would be available for torment such as the inmate from the men's camp who assisted the doctors in the infirmary where the experiments were carried out.

He was a skinny, stupid looking teenage boy with ears that stuck out from under his tattered cap. In reality, he was not much younger than Ingrid, but watched her like an old sage judging her from afar. The stare had earned him a slash from another guard's whip as they marched a road crew outside the camp. One of the SS officers Ingrid dated later held the boy down while she put out a cigarette on his bony shoulder. After that he quit looking at her.

Eighteen months after passing the guard training at Ravensbrück Ingrid Brecht was transferred to Auschwitz courtesy of her old friend Mandel who was now Lagerfuhrerin at the camp in Poland. Ingrid had a great future with the Nazis.

Ten

2006
Colorado

It was November and the town of Wildsprings, Colorado was seeing the first snowflakes gently drifting down from gray clouds to cover the ground. The retired doctor liked to walk around the town and the country lanes surrounding it regardless of the weather. Anna loved rain and snow and after strolling through it would return home to sit before a roaring fire and sip hot chocolate in her rocking chair.

As she approached her house the doctor saw a strange car in her driveway and a man in a gray frock coat on her porch. He saw Anna and waved as he descended the steps to greet her. It was Saturday, so she had no idea of who the man could be.

"Dr. Mendel?" He asked, though it was not a question.

The man was clean shaven, about forty with wavy graying hair and brown eyes. He was only medium height, but had the bearing of a man with authority or wealth, probably both.

"Yes, I'm Anna Mendel. How can help you?"

His face broke out into a smile as he offered his hand. "I'm Michael Eisen. I'm an attorney from Wichita, Kansas. Sorry to bother you on a weekend, but I have something rather urgent to discuss with you."

Anna felt her heart do a sickening thud as she recalled the newspaper article. "Is this about Ingrid?"

"Yes, I hope you can spare some time." Eisen stated, trying to read the women's response in her features.

She studied him for a moment noticing that the snow piled up on his straight shoulders as if he were a statue. "Yes, of course. Come on in." Anna led the way, dreading the topic of conversation, her pleasant afternoon suddenly ruined.

Eisen sat near the fire as Anna made coffee and placed raspberry scones on a flowered plate. He opened a briefcase and retrieved a tape recorder and a note pad in preparation for their interview. She watched him through the ornate glass that separated the living room from the kitchen until she could postpone the chat no longer.

Placing the tray with two coffee cups and the plate of scones on a table between her rocking chair and the recliner Eisen sat in, Anna pointed to cream and sugar. He nodded at the packets of creamer.

"What do you want, Mr. Eisen?" Anna asked as she stirred the coffee then handed him the cup.

"Ingrid needs your testimony or she will be deported. I cannot imagine what you must think of me even being here, much less asking for your help. I have no doubt Ingrid will be sent back to Germany, but as her lawyer I have to try to present a defense." Eisen put his pen down on the pad.

"If she is going to be deported then what good is my testimony?" The doctor inquired softly.

"Ingrid is very ashamed of her past and has spent the past fifty years as a rabbi's wife. I don't think she has any real hope of staying here, but she does want people to know that the young woman who was a camp guard has not existed for a long time. The hearing will be a record of the good she has done along with the bad." He saw Anna drift off to the past as she stared at the flames.

It had taken the doctor many years to watch chimney smoke with anything but horror. At first she had resisted using the fireplace because it kept bringing images of the camp ovens to the present. The smell was such that Anna had no doubt the locals had to have known what the Nazis were doing. "Ingrid was my best friend, Mr. Eisen. You can't imagine the struggle I've had with this since I saw the newspaper article."

"She really is different than the woman the witnesses are describing. I've been a criminal defense attorney for twenty years and most of the time I do not believe my clients ever change, but I just cannot see the evil woman being described in the one that sat across from my desk. Ingrid is a rare exception in my line of work." Eisen tried to convince her, realizing he was actually being earnest.

"I never knew why I was released. I was beaten senseless by a kapo who was always trying to impress the Aufseherin. I had given up actually and never expected to leave the infirmary. I have vague memories of being held by someone in a uniform who was crying. I was so shocked and scared, but I couldn't stay awake long enough to see her face...so it was Ingrid." Anna's eyes grew moist as she recalled the wool material against her face and the strong arms squeezing her tight.

"Yes. She was turned in by another kapo also looking to move up the ladder. As I understand it, kapos were inmates who supervised other inmates for the Nazis?" He asked while taking notes.

"Some of them were worse than the guards! It never ceases to amaze me what human ambition can make people do. They were a disgusting lot." Anna's tone had hardened.

"Did you ever see Ingrid at Ravensbrück?" Eisen looked up from the legal pad.

"No, but there were many guards and I worked at Seimens, the electrical plant there. I spent long hours working there in quality control and accounting, so I was rarely in the main camp. I have read about Ingrid being one of the guards with a dog. I am disappointed in her, but not surprised." Anna shook her head.

The lawyer straightened up at her statement. He could not have her saying that in court. "Why do you say that?

"There are leaders and followers in this world and the Nazis knew how to hook the latter. She was always fascinated by the colorful uniforms, flags, songs and the general hoopla of the Third Reich. Ingrid was by no means an exception, but rather the rule. She always looked to me to explain things. She wasn't stupid, but not an intellect either. After I was arrested and sent to a labor camp I never returned to Berlin. I don't know what happened to her after 1942. I imagine her stepfather had a great deal of sway with her after I left." The doctor sipped the hot coffee carefully.

"She told me that Ernst Brecht was a tyrant that often beat her mother, but that after she was recruited by the SS life became much more pleasant. He got a job out of it too, so it seems he was proud of her then." Eisen remarked.

"I can see where it would mean something to Ingrid to have some praise rather than being criticized and ridiculed all the time. Ernst was a drunk and her poor mother just took the shit he passed out. German women didn't have much choice then though. Careers for women involved pumping out kids for Hitler." Anna replied sourly.

Thinking about Nazi Germany was something Anna did very infrequently as she lost most her family to the camps. Her father was killed in the Berlin jail after being tortured by Gestapo thugs who received a tip that he was working against the Reich and the German people. Anna knew it was the group of Brown Shirts who had chased them and that the brick she threw had cost John Mendel his life.

"I remember Ingrid when we were little girls who liked to play together, eat at each other's houses, sleep over, you know. Down deep she was a good person, but there are some people who just have to fit in, have to be with the popular crowd regardless of who they may be. I can tell you that she loved the uniforms and if offered one Ingrid would have taken it. She simply did not see the same evil in the Nazis that I did." Anna put her cup down and leaned on her knees.

"So if she were expected to brutalize prisoners Ingrid would have done it?" Eisen felt his defense slip away. Americans typically didn't want to hear the old; *I was just following orders excuse.*

Anna studied the colorful oval rug under the coffee table as she made herself think of the past. It had a hypnotic effect as she spiraled back to Germany. "Yes, but many did. Unless you lived through the Nazi regime it's hard to understand. You got nowhere unless you were a party member. You could easily be turned in by a neighbor, friend, family member for voicing unpopular opinions. So many people disappeared who did not come back. The world looks back with hindsight and judges everyone. The Germans had to be cruel people, the Jews stupid and compliant, but the Nazis did things slowly and legally. Americans should heed the warnings I'm seeing here now. Don't ever think it couldn't happen here." Anna began to get angry.

"I'm sorry to make you think about all this. I can tell it's something you put to bed long ago." Eisen wanted to steer the conversation back to Ingrid's good deed. "You said you worked at the Seimen's plant at Ravensbrück? How did you end up at Auschwitz?"

"I worked with the a resistance group after escaping from the labor camp and continued those efforts at Seimen's by using sabotage and misinformation. When I was caught I refused to give up anyone else and was beat to a pulp for my loyalty. I was sent to Auschwitz to be worked and starved to death. It would have happened as planned if Ingrid had not heard I was in the infirmary." Anna's voice quivered.

"You were held by this person but did not see her face?" The lawyer was curious.

Anna, thinking she was being judged popped out her left eye making the man jump. "This side of my face was toward her and I was in and out of consciousness! The bitch that put me in the infirmary jabbed out my eye with a stick. This is only a high stakes poker game to you. Lawyers twist everything around to suit their own purposes. I lived that nightmare that's trotted across the history channel and set up in museum exhibits. What exactly do you want from me, Mr. Eisen?"

"I see the same Ingrid you knew sixty years ago. I also know people very well, doctor. I have to in my line of work, and I can see that you cared for Ingrid very much or it would not hurt so bad to find out the truth about her. I know she did unforgiveable things and I'm not asking you to understand or overlook them. I only want to you testify to the Ingrid you knew and how you were rescued from Auschwitz." He put the notepad on the coffee table. "Despite the enormous amount of good works Ingrid has done there are not many people coming forward to help her, especially after her poor husband died from a heart attack. They all assume it was from the strain of finding out his wife was a Nazi. I don't have much to work with here."

"Why did you take such a case?" Anna leaned back in the rocking chair and making direct eye contact.

He uncrossed his legs to let the blood flow back into joints aching from the cold weather. "I don't need the publicity or the money, Dr. Mendel. We belong to the same synagogue and I've seen what kind of person Ingrid is now. To tell you the truth I find it hard to believe we are talking about the same person. If she had denied being Ingrid Brecht I would have believed that this was a case of mistaken identity, but she did not lie about it Anna."

He watched the old woman look out the bay window behind him to watch the large snowflakes turn the landscape into a white fantasy world void of ugliness.

"I lost my partner a short time ago. We'd planned on spending our retirement traveling and enjoying the free time we worked our whole lives earning. Cancer put an end to that dream. I've been feeling sorry for myself I'll be honest, wondering what in the hell I have done to deserve this, and then you come along stirring the pot some more. I can't give you an answer now." She brought her gaze back to the visitor.

"Do you want to see her?" He asked softly.

The notion had not occurred to Anna, Ingrid being only a shadow from the distant past. "What?"

"Meet her again and then decide. She will accept whatever you want to do, but yours is the only name she gave me that matters to her. You pick the place and time." As the lawyer waited for her answer the fire popped loudly for effect.

"I guess I just assumed she was in jail." Anna stated.

"No, she is no flight risk and no danger to anyone. Her children put up her bail, which was substantial. Ingrid lives in a small apartment in Wichita. She put their house on the market right after the Rabbi's death."

"A Rabbi's wife, how the hell did that happen?" Anna shook her head and laughed.

"Ask her yourself?" Eisen smiled.

Eleven

1943-1945

Auschwitz, Poland

The first impression Ingrid Brecht had of the Auschwitz complex was that it was hell on earth. The sky always seemed gray over the three camps that made up Auschwitz I, II and III. There was always coldness to the place even in summer. The dreariness alone defeated a person upon coming through the gate and most guards felt it was a punishment being assigned there. For Ingrid it was a chance to be a supervisor, to manage and control hundreds of people, a position she was unlikely to ever posses otherwise and would not have if Maria Mandel had not befriended her.

One of her assignments was to move the women held at Auschwitz I to Auschwitz II at Birkenau. The women were housed in what had originally been constructed as horse stables. New bath houses had been built, but hardly enough for the large numbers of prisoners who had to walk naked from their wooden barracks to the bath house to wash regardless of the weather. The latrines were little more than cement holes with a roof over them and the washrooms covered troughs. The newer wood barracks had containers at both ends for excrement that putrefied the air

It was becoming harder for Brecht to watch the humiliation of mothers and grandmothers making the trek from the lice-infested rat holes they now called home just to wash. Visions of Gretchen Brecht trying to hide her breasts and vagina from the jeering SS troops drove her to soak her pesky conscious in beer much like her stepfather.

The new wood barracks in sectors BII and BIII quickly became vermin infested and acted as giant Petri dishes with only small skylights on both sides of the roof to let in light, but little fresh air. The three tiered wood bunks usually had paper stuffed mattresses that attracted mice to accompany the fleas and lice.

Ingrid was sometimes a block leader at night that dreaded entering the dreary, suffocating buildings stuffed to overflowing with prisoners. Kapos did that job for her unless there was some pressing issue that forced Ingrid inside. She preferred being outside during the day where prisoners doing manual labor could be beaten for laziness, sneezing without permission or even wetting herself. They had called this extra bit of cruelty at Ravensbrück, *Schadenfreude* or malicious pleasure.

Deep down inside Ingrid knew she was not the vicious bitch the SS expected her to be, so the booze helped boost her courage as did the admiration of the other guards. She had heard that the only woman more beautiful or meaner than Ingrid Brecht at Auschwitz was Irma Grese. She was an overseer of a punishment detail who often defied SS orders and carried unauthorized weapons such as whips. Ingrid had reached a point of no return and she knew it. It was eating a hole in her from the inside out.

Auschwitz was a miserable shithole compared to Ravensbrück and Ingrid wished that she had never been transferred there, promotion or not. Anger and misery helped fuel the passion necessary to torment and subdue the inmates. When she wasn't overseeing prisoners Ingrid was sleeping with various SS officers after an evening of drinking herself into a stupor. This behavior was typical after a hard day working in a concentration camp and it was expected that Aryans should at least make the attempt at procreation.

She was always torn between memories of her life in Berlin and the career Ingrid felt she had with the Nazi government. Known to no one but Aufseherin Brecht, there was a small picture of a Jewish girl sewn into the black uniform Lagerfuhrerin Mandel had made for her. Ingrid had no explanation of why she did not throw the photograph away as it haunted her and could earn her severe discipline if anyone found out. Somehow it seemed to keep her from going over the edge; the serious brown eyes peered through the wool fabric and chastised Ingrid for being a beast and a few women were saved from more brutal treatment.

Auschwitz existed in a time warp where minutes passed like hours, hours like days and days like months. Ingrid forgot whatever ambitions she had once had as a teenager and only hoped to stash away enough money for a decent start after the war, which no one doubted the German's would win.

After Maria Mandel was transferred to head up another camp, Ingrid was both depressed and vitalized. She missed her friend, but also felt more of a leader with Maria gone. It was around this time that a new kapo began to idolize her and imitate Brecht to the point of irritation. For some reason this woman, Elsa Frister, brought out distain in Ingrid rather than flattery. Or did Elsa make living with herself harder with a mirror image following Ingrid around?

The woman's behavior made Brecht feel foolish and ashamed, making it all the more difficult to maintain her position as she walked around the frozen compound in early December 1944. There was panic in the compound as the Russians were near, so inmates were being marched to other locations and gassings increased. The Final Solution had to continue before the Allies could stop it. The energy in the frigid air gave Ingrid a morale boost until an old high school friend took her aside one day.

Captain Heinz Gruber was also having second thoughts about their mission to clean Europe of Jews and had no illusions about who was going to win the war. SS personnel were already being tried and executed for war crimes in the east. As he went through the infirmary rounding up prisoners for transport he noticed a familiar face, even though it was bruised and battered with an eye gouged out. It was an old classmate he had once liked and teased, Anna Mendel.

He told Ingrid that a kapo named Frister had injured Anna and returned to the infirmary to burn her initials into Anna's shoulder with a cigarette. Ingrid's heart sank as she had hoped the Mendel's had somehow escaped Hitler's Germanic purge.

When she found Anna in the dank, vermin infested infirmary Ingrid lost control and for the first time the prisoners became human for her. After holding and comforting her friend or nearly twenty minutes, to the shock of those well enough to notice, Ingrid had Anna transferred to the SS hospital. She was not questioned as overseer Brecht told the medical staff that Anna was not Jewish, but an Aryan who was a mechanical engineer. Such talent was not to be wasted in the Reich's now desperate struggle against the Allies.

Heinz had a woman he was having a fling with in administration falsify release forms for Anna Mendel and Ingrid signed them along with him. Gruber then went on a death march and was captured by the Russians while trying to get inmates far away from Auschwitz.

A furious Ingrid found Frister in the middle of a snowy night and beat her to a bloody pulp with an ax handle. Her superiors soon discovered her treachery and made her strip before the inmates of her block and put on the regulation striped dress. She then received her own tattooed prisoner number and was thrown in with those she had tormented for three weeks before the Russians liberated the camp. Ingrid had told U.S. Immigration that she was an inmate for three months, a lie that she felt was inconsequential as it was a horrible three weeks. Showing compassion for one woman was not enough to compensate for the cruelty Ingrid had shown in her stint as a Nazi guard.

In the chaos of January 1945 when the Russians invaded the camp, Ingrid Brecht managed to blend in with newly arrived prisoners who did not know her and was trucked off to a Red Cross camp where she was fed and cared for until resettling in a rural community in the Alps. She then immigrated to America in 1948 as Ingrid Goldstein. It was the name the SS gave her when assigning the number to further humiliate her, but in the end it aided in her escape.

Twelve

1946 to 2006

The United States

Anna Mendel also immigrated to the United States to live with a cousin and attended Harvard University where she was at last allowed to shine. It was a difficult journey where the tremendous pain of her past was never far away. But she ploughed into her studies and graduated Summa Cum Laude, earning a spot in the medical school.

In some ways Anna felt like a freak being a survivor of something that was impossible to describe to ordinary people. The full story of the camps and Nazi Europe was only beginning to be told and it would be decades before the whole story would come out. Americans simply had no concept of the horror lived in the Nazi concentration camps.

There were accusations that Jews had made no attempt to fight back and were just led off to the slaughter house, but Anna would lash out at times in defense of her family and friends now lying in unmarked graves or were long vanished incinerator smoke. She reluctantly gave talks in local synagogues and churches where people were shocked and sickened by the treatment of Jews and others deemed subhuman, but found little solace. How could people have not known what was going on in Europe? Maybe the common people had no clue, but the politicians did-of that Anna had no doubt.

The torment Anna felt daily she molded into passion for Harvard medical school. She had the talent and intelligence for surgery, but chose to practice internal medicine. Anna had no desire to make a fortune. She wanted to cure illness and restore health and hopefully heal herself in the process.

After residency at Johns Hopkins where Anna saw patients from every walk of life, she heard about a town called Wildsprings in Colorado. Another resident who had no desire to return to a small town told her that the town doctor was retiring and looking for someone to replace him. Dr. Mendel fell in love with the town and made it her life's work.

For decades Anna delivered babies, treated colds and mended broken bones in a place where crime was nearly unheard of except for school boy pranks. She put Nazi Germany far behind her and pushed memories of that time into a dark recess of her mind, wearing long sleeve shirts to avoid talking about the number carved into her arm.

Anna also left religion in the past making no attempt to connect with Jewish communities in America. She wanted a whole new start and being a "Holocaust survivor" was not the way to start over. The local veterinarian had been in Treblinka, but Anna had avoided her the first five years in Wildsprings, unwilling to have any link with that kind of suffering and injustice.

Then one day a horse reared up and brought a hoof down on the woman's forearm causing a hairline fracture in the ulna. It forced Agnes Eichel to seek medical help when she usually prescribed her own treatments.

Unlike Anna, Eichel had no problem reminding the world about Hitler and the Nazis. She was very active in survivor groups that sought to educate children about the dangers of a dictatorship and the inaction that allows them to be created. Agnes still spoke German, which at first disturbed some of the World War II veterans in town, but her personality and generosity overcame any reservations people held against Germans.

Anna only wanted to build a new life, a whole new chapter independent of life in Germany and she avoided the pretty charming woman from Bavaria who suddenly made doctor's appointments for every sniffle. Agnes was funny and sought after by several of the town's bachelors, but she only had eyes for the serious, quiet general practitioner who lived alone at the edge of town.

Loss was so devastating to the heart that Anna resisted falling in love. She had lost her immediate family to the camps and knew how swiftly and unexpectedly people could vanish from a person's life, leaving a cold, hollow void where warmth once dwelled.

Agnes persisted though, coming by the house to talk while Anna worked in her garden. The contents of the picnic basket she brought came to be a surprise Anna looked forward to on the weekends. Sometimes it was German delights like Kartoffelknödel (potato dumplings) or Cheese-spaetzle, or American treats such as fried chicken and apple pie.

They took comfort in each other during the Korean War wondering with dread when the next regime would take over and then Vietnam emerged as a controversial "police action" that again made them nervous. War seemed always hovering over the world and as time passed Anna was glad to have Agnes at her side. Gradually life became enjoyable as the past grew further behind them and the two women found peace and happiness.

Then thirty-five years later Agnes began to have sharp stabbing pains in her side, which did not alert Anna at first because Agnes had pleurisy, an inflammation of the chest lining that could be quite painful. She then quickly tired easily and began to have blood in her stools. Anna ran tests and found tumors in the liver from colon cancer. The doctor was shocked and angry that she had not caught the disease before it had so advanced. Chemotherapy had only shrunk the tumors temporarily and the cancer returned with a vengeance. Not even the insurmountable Agnes beat cancer.

Agnes Eichel now lay in the Wildsprings cemetery where snow fell on her headstone bearing the statement, "A Survivor of Treblinka." She flipped off the Nazis even in death. Anna Mendel stood over the snow covered grave where she had placed white roses, a tribute to their favorite German resistance group. The White Rose was headed by Hans and Sophie Scholl, brother and sister students in Munich who were beheaded for distributing anti-Nazi pamphlets.

If only Agnes were here with her now. The coldness that made Anna shiver had nothing to do with the wintery environment. She would live out the rest of her life alone and face the ordeal with Ingrid Brecht without the strong, positive influence of her partner. Anna cursed God and not for the first time.

She could just ignore the request to meet and talk with Ingrid, a very unwelcomed ghost from the past. Yes, her old friend had helped Anna escape and survive, but what of the hundreds Ingrid had abused and tortured? Did one act of kindness erase such guilt? A Rabbi's wife? It was almost a joke considering the attitude of Ernst Brecht toward Jews and the lack of any religious conviction in the family. What a crock of shit! Anna didn't even belong to a synagogue and yet Ingrid had converted and served the Jewish community for fifty years.

The quiet woody landscape brought back visions of the Berlin Tiergarten where she once rode bikes with Ingrid and other childhood friends. It was a beautiful bit of countryside within a major city, once the royal hunting grounds of Friedrich Wilhelm. The park had been destroyed by Allied bombing before the Nazis could turn it into something vile. What would the future have been like with no Hitler?

It was not healthy to think in such a manner. There was nothing Anna could do about the past, no way to undo the tragedy that fell like oozing pitch all over Europe. Where was God when that demon ruined so many lives and destroyed an ancient and proud culture? And it was destroyed. Germany would never be the same again. It would take centuries more for the stain of Nazism to fade from a still stinging memory.

What would Agnes say about Ingrid? Anna knew that she would tell her to face the woman who was once her best friend. They had both known people in the Hitler Youth or members of the Nazi Party as it was impossible not to at the time. Many people had joined without committing atrocities. Agnes would not expect her to forgive or forget, but confront Ingrid and get some answers as to what happened.

Anna sighed as tears ran down her chilled cheeks. They had both suffered so much and then had given their entire lives to helping people and animals. All they had asked in return was to spend their remaining years traveling together and enjoying life. Instead, Agnes got a headstone and Anna was left alone in a frigid graveyard with the devil breathing down her neck. Anger replaced sorrow as snowflakes drifted down and covered the roses. Ingrid wanted sympathy? She would get none from Dr. Anna Mendel.

Thirteen

2006

Kansas

Everyone at the apartment complex off of Webb Road knew why garbage had been thrown on Ingrid Levy's doorstep. The same reason scorching, obscene graffiti had been spray painted on her car. Her attorney suggested that Ingrid find somewhere else to live outside of Wichita and found her a small house in Augusta, Kansas just north of Wichita.

One of her former neighbors had growled at her, "Was it worth it you Nazi bitch?" The young man was tall, blonde and blue eyed and Ingrid wanted to retort, but reframed from starting a shouting match. Did he think he was beyond the influences of colorful flags and parades? *I was like you once you little smart ass!*

Fortunately, the younger generation knew little about German history and cared even less. Soon most forgot about Ingrid Levy, the former camp guard and no one in the small town seemed to recognize the old lady that rented a small house on State Street. She was already old news.

But it wasn't the reaction of strangers that tore at Ingrid. Her son and daughter seemed to be in shock after finding out that their mother was a cruel Nazi camp guard. They had initially hoped that the witnesses had mixed their mother up with someone else, but those hopes were dashed when Ingrid did not deny being Ingrid Brecht and admitted that she was with the SS auxiliary.

Her children, David and Sarah, lived in the Chicago area and tried to convince her to move back there to be near them. It made sense to be closer to her support group, but Ingrid could not face people who knew her as the rabbi's wife. She hovered between being ashamed of the past and defensive. Why should she still have to explain herself fifty years later for something she had done as a young woman?

Perhaps she should have denied being Ingrid Brecht. It would have been hard to prove with Nazi camp records matching her number to Ingrid Goldstein. She could have just said the witnesses were mistaken as hardly anyone knew the names of the women guards. It was a long time ago and the witnesses had been under a great deal of stress. Her lawyer could have spun circles around the elderly people accusing a rabbi's wife of war crimes.

Americans acted like they were above being drawn into a movement like the Nazis, but if it were not for the support of American corporations Hitler would never have been in power or been able to arm Germany to such an extent. The world had been fooled by the excitement of a new Germany the same as Germans. No one had wanted to believe the sinister intentions of Hitler and his henchmen. One should never under estimate the power of denial.

When sitting in her small backyard at a round patio table with a striped umbrella in the center, Ingrid was propelled back to Berlin when she first became part of the Nazi movement. Was she proud of her involvement? Hell yes! She was a member of the SS auxiliary, had met the same strict requirements of the male SS members. Mingling with important people bound for greatness was intoxicating for a girl of eighteen who sipped beer in outside taverns called Biergartens with SS officers.

The next door neighbors had cooked outside on a barbeque grill and now sat at a picnic table eating hotdogs. She could see the family of four through the slits in the wood fence. The boy and girl ate cheerfully with mustard and ketchup on their faces, swinging their feet without a care in the world. The parents chatted and laughed as they heaped mounds of condiments on their hotdogs.

Ingrid and Anna had once sat outside the restaurant, Zum Naussbaum in Berlin at a table with a green and white checkered cloth like the one covering the neighbor's table. They too laughed and chatted with each other and Gretchen Brecht who had taken them on a day trip. The girls were about eight years old then. It was one of Ingrid's most cherished memories. If only she could dial back the clock and eliminate Hitler from history how many more warm moments could there have been?

While taunts and jabs from people regarding her past stung greatly, what Ingrid found more disturbing were the emails she received from Aryan groups offering their support and wanting details about being a Nazi serving the Reich. Pictures attached to the emails revealed young men with the same proud gleam in their eyes that she recalled from her youth. Was she always to be aligned with the Nazis? If you planted hemlock as a child did it taint any sweet grapes you might plant as an adult?

Even worse were the Holocaust deniers who assumed that she would endorse their cause. Ingrid replied that they were fools and did not understand the true Nazi mentality. No real Nazi would ever deny what Hitler had worked so hard to accomplish. It was a matter of pride and accomplishment and certainly a devotee would never say it did not happen. Ingrid had been in the midst of it all and damned well knew it to be true.

As Ingrid smiled at the young family next door her cell phone rang. It was Eisen, her attorney. Dr. Mendel refused to meet with Ingrid and would not be a character witness. Until that moment she had not realized how very much she had wanted to see Anna.

"Listen Ingrid, you have decades of honorable service to the Jewish community. Your reputation as an American citizen far outshines anything you did in Germany. Even if you lose, I can appeal for years and you more than likely will never be deported." Eisen paused as he heard quiet sobs. "I know how much you wanted to make peace with Anna, but you may just have to be content with the knowledge that she is alive because of your actions."

"You're right, of course. As far as Anna is concerned I killed her whole family and her way of life. I made my bed when I put that uniform on." She felt her identity as Mrs. Levy falling off like chipped paint to reveal Ingrid Brecht who had been there all along.

"I see no point to you losing your citizenship or being deported to Germany. No one condones what you did in the camps, but I did some stupid, mean and even illegal things just to fit in with my fraternity. I understand the pressure you were under as I was expected to follow my father's path and, quite frankly, I had no choice in the matter. I was simply too weak to face the consequences of failure." When recalling the superiority he had felt when dealing with frightened pledges, he remembered no flickers of sympathy though Eisen had suffered the same only two years earlier.

"I guess many of us regret the past, Mr. Eisen." Ingrid replied, thankful for his support.

"We all do things that are expected at the time or considered rites of passage. I honestly don't know how I would have responded as a half Jew in Germany. My mother was Catholic and I may well have denied my Jewish ancestry to save my ass. No matter how noble we think we are self preservation comes first for most people." The lawyer had been preparing psychologically for his client's defense both for himself and the public. Representing a former Nazi would require a stiff backbone.

"How does your wife feel about you having me as a client?" Ingrid glanced at the happy family knowing they believed Nazis were evil.

He cleared his throat. "She doesn't like it and will be quite glad when it's over. Helen cannot imagine how I could take on a former Nazi and we have argued about it many times."

"Then why do you cause yourself such problems on my behalf?" She asked.

"Because I can't reconcile that tyrant in a cape storming around Auschwitz with the woman I know now. You are proof to me that rehabilitation does happen and people do change. I've represented some real scumbags, Ingrid. Let's just say that I need to do this."

"I want an official record of my positive work since the war, but more than anything I wanted to talk with Anna again." Her voiced cracked.

"She lives in Wildsprings, Colorado on the edge of town, you can't miss it. How is it that you never tried to find her before?" He honestly wondered since it was so important to her.

"I was ashamed...and somewhat afraid she would denounce me to authorities. Anna was my conscious and intellect, and I the passion-together we made a great person. After all these years it still matters to me what she thinks." Ingrid sighed.

"Then take the chance and go see her, but be prepared for rejection. It sounds like you need to do it for your own peace of mind." Eisen recalled the quiet, but strong woman he interviewed in Colorado and was not certain how she would react to finding Ingrid Brecht in her territory.

As she hung up the phone Ingrid saw the children wave at her through the fence. The parents also looked at the handsome, dignified woman sitting at the patio table and also waved. She smiled and returned the greetings knowing that they would hide their sweet children if they knew a Nazi concentration camp guard lived next door. She was the famed *Bogeyman* of children's stories.

Fourteen

1945

Germany

Once released from Auschwitz Anna was picked up by an old couple with a wagon who took her to their farm near the Polish town of Oswiecim. Not knowing any Polish and being too weak to argue she went to their small house where she convalesced through March. When strong enough to walk down the road she ran into a group of former inmates walking back to Germany. She never learned the identity of the farmers or why they had picked up a sickly stranger.

Anna Mendel found herself in a British refugee camp not all that different from the German ones in that it was temporary and overcrowded. The Allies had an enormous problem with millions of homeless people having nowhere to go and no income. They were also busy cleaning up the trail of corpses the Nazis had left behind and trying to control the spread of disease.

There was no forced labor and the food was actually edible, but the camp was filled with scared, stressed and starving people who needed answers and solutions not easily provided. The first miracle she experienced was hot water. The old couple had let her bathe of course, but having a hot shower and new clothes were a joy beyond description. When people are made to live like beasts for years the simplest things make the heart nearly burst with happiness.

She had surgery to remove the injured eye and until Anna immigrated to the United States she wore an eye patch over the empty socket. Every glance at a mirror or reflection angered Anna who was horrified by the hollow cheeked macabre being who stared back at her. It took two months, but Anna finally learned that she was the only survivor in her family. She got the easy end of it.

After her father was beaten to death in jail, Anna's mother and sister were sent to Bergen Belsen where they died and her brother-in-law, Bernard to Dachau. For reasons unclear he was hung three months after arriving. Knowing Bernard, Anna figured he had refused to participate in some medical experiment. The deaths of her mother and sister were listed as the natural cause of typhus. Sure, unless you considered the fact that they would never have contracted it in a thousand years living in their own homes unmolested by Nazi thugs.

Anna volunteered at a hospital in Berlin after assisting the Red Cross at the British camp. She learned nursing skills that would benefit her during and after medical school. The Nazis had provided a crash course in a multitude of disease and injury studies unsurpassed in modern history. Thousands of people who had managed to live to be liberated died from kindness in that their ravaged systems could not handle solid food or it was simply too late to stop the death clock. The psychological damage was indescribable and for many permanent.

Most of the inhabitants of Berlin at the war's end were women and children. The horror continued when Anna had to treat thousands of rape victims and those begging for information about how to commit suicide. The Russian soldiers raped even eight year old girls in the streets. Nearly anyone who wanted to survive ended up some soldier's mistress for food and protection. The alternative was gang rape and death.

In the American sector in southwest Berlin things were not much better as anything German, including the women, were considered war booty. Germans deserved to be punished forever and if not for her obvious camp tattoo Anna would have been raped as well. The Americans thought that since they traded canned meat or a bar of soap for sex it was not really rape and troops were supplied with a steady stream of condoms. When the Americans troops were allowed to bring their wives to Germany they were issued uniforms to keep them safe.

Anna became friends with an American officer's wife, Carol Andersen, who gave her a copy of a book entitled, *Germany is our Problem* by the American Secretary of State, Henry Morgenthau. It was disturbing that foreign policy was being based on his viewpoints that included starvation rations for German citizens and sterilization. Nothing would be said about it because many believed retaliation was justified for allowing the Nazis to run the country. But what about the innocent?

One day Anna's supervisor tracked her down with a message from the Red Cross that a cousin in America was searching for family that had survived the war. Ashley Hering lived in Boston and was willing to sponsor whoever might be willing to immigrate. She was actually a second cousin born in America that had never met Anna Mendel.

It seemed ironic that she had the opportunity to flee Berlin when it was now a ragged, ghostly shell of piled rubble and bleak stone skeletons. When it would have done the most good to leave the Mendel's did not and now a young Anna would embark on a new journey alone.

There was little left in her family's shop, but Anna did manage to find some photographs and ledgers with her father's handwriting on a store room shelf. Looters had ravaged the shop and bombs finished it off. Anything of value had been stolen or destroyed by the bombing. The same was true of their apartment building where Anna gathered a few personal items. Remnants of her past life fit into one small wooden box.

A note was pinned to the living room wall with the address of an elderly great aunt and uncle who had fled to Belgium in 1932. It was meant for any family member who might stumble back to Berlin. Anna took it and planned to write them once in America. She was too numb to deal with the nightmare of the past twelve years and wanted as far away from Germany as possible. They had waited all that time for news, so the Meier's could wait one more month while Anna sailed to Boston.

Even if the apartment had not been nearly destroyed Anna could not have lived there again. There was no going back for her. She did stand across the street from the Brecht apartment for a short while, but saw no sign of life. What would she have said to them anyway? A poster that looked like Ingrid in a SS uniform was still stuck to a wall. Anna stared in disbelief. Exactly what had her old friend done for the Nazis?

The Russians had German civilians cleaning up the tons of rubble that littered the streets and they were none too friendly about it either. Anna had to admit that she enjoyed watching those who had condemned her family to death be chastised and humiliated by foreigners. Let them haul off the trash and rebuild Berlin, Anna wanted the hell out.

The American soldiers that saw the number branded into her arm nodded in respect or asked if Anna needed help. They never asked her to grab a shovel or haul rubble, but she was not sure if it had to do with her former camp status or the fact that she was so thin manual labor appeared out of the question.

So what did Hitler's followers think of their thousand year Reich now? Rather than restore German pride the Nazis had murdered, stolen, tortured and embarrassed Germans for decades to come. A once beautiful and majestic country now lay in piles of broken stones, was littered with mass graves and clouds filled with human ashes floated over the Fatherland.

Many would remain to put the pieces of a shattered Germany back together, but Anna had not met many Jews who planned on staying. The wounds were deep, infected and not easily cured. She felt betrayed by a land that only a short time ago had no problem allowing patriotic Jewish soldiers to die for the cause, then loaded up box cars with the same people as fodder for its blazing ovens.

It seemed at times that the nightmare would never end with reminders of the recent horror in pained expressions, fallen structures and wasted landscapes. Even on sunny days Berlin was dull and gray with the remnants of Nazi flags being the only hints of color. Hell could not possibly be any worse than the world the Nazis had created.

Fifteen

2006

Colorado

The late winter sky was clear blue with fluffy white clouds floating about like cotton balls as Anna walked down the main street of Wildsprings. After two years of being on the market, Agnes's veterinary practice would once again be up and running. She was very particular about the type of person taking over as vet and left it up to Anna to find a good replacement for Wildsprings.

The nod had gone to a young man of thirty named Peter Kline who had only been practicing for three years, but Anna was sure Agnes would have liked him. He had no plans to redecorate the clinic and thought her filing system was superior. Kline would simply pick up where Agnes left off. They would finalize the paperwork the coming week, but Anna gave him the keys so Peter could begin moving in.

She felt good as she walked the few blocks through town toward home. The local café was busy and the smell of the Tuesday special drifted out into the street. Chip and Barb Newsom were well known for their meatloaf, fresh mashed potatoes and bettered corn on the cob, including many of her heart patients, but even Anna had to admit the food was hard to resist although a cardiac disaster.

Not wanting to cook anything for dinner Anna entered the lively restaurant where she was greeted warmly. She slid into an empty booth next to the retired postmaster, Jim McSorley and his wife.

He turned around to face her. "Hey Anna, there was a lady asking about you earlier. Wouldn't give her name though, just said she was an old acquaintance."

"Probably an old patient." Anna didn't give it much thought as it wasn't unusual for babies she had delivered to come calling in adulthood or for those who had moved away to stop by while in the area.

"She asked where you lived and I pointed your place out, hope that was okay?" Jim asked although it was too late to remedy the situation. His wife smirked at Anna who laughed as if to say, *now he asks!*

"I'm sure nothing will come of it." Anna remarked as the waitress leaned against the table with an order book. "I'll have the special and ice tea." Anna told her.

The café was decorated in 1950s style and still had a counter with stools and a soda fountain. People on day trips often came there for lunch, particularly bikers from around the state out for joy rides.

Anna smiled as she took in the scents of cheeseburgers and fries, the homey aromas of small town America. She was pleased to have sold Agnes' business and finally able to look forward to finding happiness in her retirement-happiness she had earned through surviving the camps and working hard for years. Agnes would want her to move on and not dwell on her early death.

As Anna leisurely ate supper a silvery haired woman sat in a rented white Lincoln Towncar studying the doctor's house. Blood rushed through her ears as a nervous heart pounded against her sternum. Ingrid did not know Dr. Mendel, only the shadowy memory of the woman as a child. Anna didn't want to see her and already stated that she would not help her. So *what was she doing there?*

Half an hour later Ingrid saw an older thin woman walking up the street in the rear view mirror. She wore a tee shirt and jeans with a light wind breaker, hands jammed into pockets casually strolling in the late afternoon sun. She seemed happy. When it was clear that the woman was heading toward Anna's house Ingrid panicked and drove off.

Dr. Mendel shrugged it off. It was probably a drug representative as many of them were either were not aware that she had retired or knew that she covered for the new physician when he was out of town and tried to hunt her down. More than likely it was the same woman who was looking for her earlier.

She finished off the day with an evening of movies and popcorn in her living room, the only interruption coming from an unknown number with the caller hanging up when Anna answered the phone.

Several days Anna later found a cement bench placed near Agnes' grave. *Who had bought it?* While it could have been any number of her friends or former patients, the doctor felt a foreboding about the gift and wondered if there was a connection with the stranger. She scanned the area around the wooded graveyard, but saw no one. One the back of the bench was engraved the words, *Never Again*. It could be a reference to the Holocaust and merely a gesture of support since Agnes was an outspoken about her time at Treblinka.

The nearest monument dealer was just outside of Denver about an hour away. When Anna called them to inquire about who purchased the bench she was told that the donor was anonymous. A woman had paid in cash and simply stated that she too was a camp survivor. It was Ingrid, of that Anna now had no doubt. *What the hell would she do about it?*

The local sheriff was an old friend and patient, John Beecher. She knocked on the door of the small cottage type house he shared with his wife, Noreen. The middle aged couple was happy to see her. They were ready to slice into a freshly baked apple pie when Anna came to visit.

The Beecher's were aware of Anna's past and her recent visit from Ingrid's lawyer. She wanted their advice and their opinions regarding the situation.

"I don't blame you for not wanting to see her or testify for her, Anna." Noreen remarking as she slid a piece of pie onto a plate for their guest. "I can't even imagine how I feel."

John got up from the table to retrieve vanilla ice cream from the freezer. "Ice cream?" He asked the two women who quickly agreed.

"So Ingrid bought a bench for Agnes' grave? Kind of a bribe you think?" John speculated as he plopped a scoop of ice cream onto Anna's plate.

"I don't know, John. I made it clear that I did not want to meet with her, but she comes here anyway. I'm not sure that it is an attempt to convince me to testify, the Ingrid I remember would have done it because she was sorry for being stupid. She never did have much of a mind of her own." Anna poked her pie with a long fork.

Noreen appeared concerned. "Maybe she is? I know that the paper said she did horrible things, but also did many good things since she's been here. I'm sorry; I don't mean that I feel sympathy for her."

"You could have the company come pick it up, that would send Ingrid a message." John took a bite of the pie saturated with ice cream and it clung to his blond mustache.

"Yes, and you would have every right to do to." Noreen nodded, somewhat relieved that her husband had taken a hard approach.

Anna looked to Noreen. "But you think I should talk to her?

"I wonder if you could have some closure, Anna. You are hurt and angry, perhaps you need to let Ingrid know how you feel about her behavior and maybe you need to hear her explain why she did it? If my best friend joined the Nazis I'd damned well want to know why." Noreen's ash brown hair fell down into her eyes as she shook her head.

"Can I be blunt? If it didn't matter to you, Anna you would have called her lawyer and told him to tell her to fuck off. I know you and you are not shy about speaking your mind. Face her; make the woman give you some answers. She pisses you off, punch her!" He smiled.

"Can I quote you on that, Sheriff?" Anna winked at Noreen. "I did care for her once, very much. I guess it's the betrayal that gets me. That she put on the uniform and stabbed my family in the back." She laid her fork down. "I just wanted the past to stay there and then she had to be arrested. I almost wish to God that they had just let Ingrid alone. How selfish is that?"

"You want me to get a message to her" Beecher let out a slight belch.

"You know where she is staying?" Anna asked, surprised.

"We look out after our own here. John was just making sure that she did not cause you any trouble." Noreen patted Anna's hand.

"I saw her parked across from your house and I'd seen her driving around town before. I checked the plates and they came back to an Ingrid Levy. Since she chickened out and didn't come to the door I had no reason to stop her. She's staying at a mom and pop motel this side of Denver."

Anna Mendel chuckled and blushed at the concern of her neighbors. "Thank you, for watching out for an old woman."

"No problem, Doc." John finished up his pie.

Anna chewed slowly then drank her ice water. "Yes, tell Ingrid I will meet with her this Saturday at the cemetery and we'll sit on that bench of hers. See how she likes talking dirt on the Sabbath."

Sixteen

1948

The United States

Ingrid Brecht was one of those people who luck smiled on no matter the circumstances. The pilgrims who sailed to America centuries before her believed in a predetermined destiny in that a person's fate was already planned out before hand, so that regardless of a person's actions they were either charmed or screwed. Ingrid was charmed.

She crossed the ocean on a ship that docked in Galway to pick up Irish passengers and met the McInnes family. They were on their way to New York City where the wife's parents lived. Ian McInnes had taken a fancy to a Jewish girl and married her against fierce family opposition. They tried to raise their children in the Limerick area, but the hostility was clearly a long term situation. The wife's family, however, had no such concerns and invited them to immigrate to the United States. Iris McInnes was an only child and her parents had no qualms about their grandchildren's father being a Catholic.

Ian's family had lost all of their lands to the English and then began to starve to death when the Limeys sold all the potatoes to other countries. He was fully sympathetic to Ingrid's plight and her stories about the Nazis stealing all of her family's possessions and shipping them off to camps. The couple invited her to come with them after cabling the Daniels for permission.

Pretending to be a Jew was very easy, even though Ingrid was raised a Protestant. She knew enough from visiting the Mendel's to fit her story that her family was not very religious, but rounded up by the Nazi's anyway. It happened to thousands of other families whose Jewishness either meant nothing to them or was a complete surprise. The numbers burned into her arm were the keys to her new life. No one thought to question the brand as the young woman was a victim of the worse crime in history.

The Daniels had been basketball fans who attended games at Columbia University. A family friend played on the team while getting dual degrees from Columbia and Yeshiva University. Herschel Levy was a brilliant student and athlete whose attentions soon settled on the beautiful Ingrid Goldstein.

Herschel was fascinated by the pretty, dignified woman who had suffered so much for her legacy. He was studying to be a rabbi, which meant that either Ingrid would have to provide documentation that her mother was Jewish or convert if they were to marry. Being unwilling to have her past dug into, Ingrid suggested that she go through classes for conversion since she knew next to nothing about the Jewish religion, quite unacceptable for a rabbi's wife.

Everyone that met Ingrid felt her strength and goodness. Nothing was too much to ask of her and she was tireless when working to help others, especially on Christmas when the synagogue cooked dinner for homeless Christians with no place to go. Ingrid was the epitome of a rabbi's companion and Herschel felt blessed by God to have her.

But everyday was fearful for her, never knowing if someone would recognize her and bring the new found sanctuary walls tumbling down. As the years passed she convinced herself that the person she had been died in Germany leaving only Ingrid Levy the Holocaust survivor and pillar of the Jewish community.

When their children were born Ingrid was even more confident that her past had been forgotten and when Herschel was offered a position as head rabbi in Chicago their future seemed set. At first Ingrid was alarmed by the amount of holocaust survivors living in the area, especially from Auschwitz.

There was a close call once when a woman with dementia was brought to services from a nursing home. She was mute, but the terror in her eyes fully registered with Ingrid who nearly choked as her throat tightened in panic. The poor woman was taken home with the aide thinking the outing was too much for the old woman. Ingrid had retreated to the restroom to splash cold water in her face, thankful that the woman could not talk.

She threw herself into being the most devoted spouse any rabbi ever had, as if she could erase the Ingrid Brecht who had solicited horror from so many people at Ravensbrück and Auschwitz, the vile creature who could pour stark fear into an innocent old woman's eyes fifteen years later.

Fortunately for Ingrid, the camp inmates who would re-member her as the Auschwitz guard who was branded a Jew in 1945 lived in Florida and would not see her photograph for forty years.

Seventeen

2006
Colorado

Ingrid sat a rock in the woods near Grand Lake, Colorado. It reminded her of trips to Bavaria to visit her uncle who was a clockmaker. The air was cool and fresh, the trees green and tall, the scent of pine renewed with every breeze that tossed their branches.

If only she could will herself back to age eleven when she had her uncle make a cuckoo clock for Anna's birthday or back to camping trips with the League of German Girls where they hiked and roasted sausages outdoors. Better still Ingrid would like to time travel back to a time when she could murder that bastard Adolph before he could piss over all Europe. But that was not possible.

She wore khaki slacks and a pink shirt with a white scarf tied around her long neck. Ingrid appeared as any kindly grandmother watching children and their parents hike on the trail below her. Down deep Ingrid knew she had been given a forty year reprieve to marry and raise a family, much more that many thousands had been given by the Nazis. How many had never known love or had lost it because of her? She had already made the decision to not fight deportation back to Germany.

Her children and grandchildren would be hurt and upset, but Ingrid had to pay the piper and face the crimes she had committed. The years of happiness she had known she had not earned or deserved and accepted that fact now as she contemplated meeting her childhood friend Anna Mendel again. Anna would not be merciful, Ingrid knew. She had been one friend who would not just tell Ingrid what she wanted to hear, but only the cold hard truth.

What a tremendous fool she had been to be so terrified of her feelings for Anna, feelings that may not have been more than a schoolgirl crush and not life defining as her brother had indicated. Even at that Albert had meant no harm to the gay culture. He was merely a teenage boy trying to mess with his sister's head and Ingrid fell for it. Had Albert really died on the eastern front or had he spent decades in a Russian gulag thinking of their happier times?

Wildsprings was twenty minutes east of Grand Lake where Ingrid had found a room for the night. The area was beautiful and she hoped the atmosphere might calm her for the meeting the next day. Some would find her nervousness amusing. A tall, strong former Nazi fearful of a slight, woman of science whose idea of physical activity had been a walk or bike ride to her father's shop.

Ingrid had learned a great deal about strength and what only masqueraded as strength. The meaner a person appeared, the weaker they were inside, the faster they ran from themselves.

Self hatred propelled people to do horrendous things to avoid facing the truth. She would never under estimate the power of low self esteem or humiliation to create monsters.

That night Ingrid called her daughter and told her that she would be meeting her old friend tomorrow. Karen was concerned that her mother would be hurt by the encounter and again asked Ingrid to move back to Chicago. Rather than argue, Ingrid replied that she would think about it.

The night was long and restless at the motel with Ingrid finally giving up trying to sleep and watching some movie on cable while munching peanuts from a vending machine. She began to doze right before the sunlight shot through the curtains and jolted her awake. *Oh shit.* Before stepping into the shower Ingrid made coffee with the little pot provided by the motel. She packed slowly, folding even her dirty clothes before placing them in a string bag. After her reunion with Anna, Ingrid would return home to Wichita and tell her lawyer she was going back to Germany.

Eighteen

2006

Colorado

Anna arrived at the cemetery early and walked west toward a valley lined with graves and oak trees planted when the town was first founded. She waited for the white Towncar Ingrid had rented to pull up behind her red pickup, which it did just before nine in the morning.

A tall, white haired woman stood next to the car, searching the area for the truck's driver. Her movements were the same as Anna remembered and she pushed back a feeling of warmth and joy that shocked her. Anna leaned against a large oak until she could regain control of her emotions. This was not some high school reunion where long lost friends could rejoice and reminisce.

Ingrid sat on the bench next to Agnes' grave. She wore a white sweater over a light blue shirt with tan slacks. A brown sack from the local diner was placed next to her along with two Styrofoam cups Anna assumed was hot chocolate as they used to drink as children. In the sack were probably cinnamon bagels like Mrs. Mendel made for breakfast. This was not going to be easy and Anna now wished she had not agreed to the meeting, but she would not back out now.

As Anna walked gingerly toward her old friend, Ingrid turned right, watching her approach in silence with her hands tightly clasped. When she was near the bench Ingrid asked if she was Anna.

"I'm Anna Mendel. Ingrid?" The doctor sat down on the far end of the bench as the other woman nodded her head.

The two women studied each other almost in disbelief, neither quite sure that what was happening was real.

"I thought we might enjoy some hot chocolate and bagels....."Ingrid offered.

"I still like both, yes. Thank you." Anna looked into Ingrid's blue eyes and face, which still bore the same features she remembered so long ago.

Ingrid opened the sack and gave Anna a bagel and handed her a cup. She studied Anna's face and noticed something different in her brown eyes.

"Pardon me for mentioning it, but you have blue circles around your eyes, are you okay?" Ingrid asked softly.

Anna grinned and sipped the drink. "Ironic isn't it?" When Ingrid appeared puzzled she continued. "High cholesterol. The Nazis went to all that trouble in order to create Aryans by trying to turn brown eyes blue, and all they had to do was feed us cheese and eggs instead of starving us!"

"Oh Anna, you're still you. I know that I have no right to, but I've missed you so much." Ingrid looked down at her cup with tears forming.

"What is it you want from me, Ingrid?" Anna hooked her arm over the back of the bench to face her visitor.

"I don't honestly know. It isn't about the hearing, Anna. I've already decided to return to Germany voluntarily. I had fifty years of being a wife and mother, of being happy and now I want to know about your life after the camps. Did I do a good deed by saving you? They told you it was me didn't they? I met so many survivors who wished the hell they had died and I often thought of you, wondering where you were and what you were doing." Ingrid turned toward Anna, laying her bagel on the sack untouched.

"I figured out it was you long before anyone told me. The other inmates in the infirmary told me that a guard had held me in her arms and rocked me, crying like a baby." Anna's voice cracked and she swallowed hard. "Now what other fucking Nazi would have done that!" She sobbed and covered her face with both hands.

Ingrid began to cry as well. "I was so furious when I found out what that kapo had done to you, oh God when I saw how awful you looked I just broke down and I didn't care who saw me."

Anna reached out and took Ingrid's hand, surprising the both of them. "I've had a good life with a good woman. It was hard to get past what happened to me and my family, but I would not have been a doctor all these years if you had not saved me."

"I killed the kapo that tortured you." Ingrid stated flatly. "That is one murder of which I am directly guilty and one I am not sorry for." She looked Anna in the eyes.

"Your lawyer told me that the Nazis stripped you of your rank and made you one of us. You spent months as an inmate, but if you were really sorry for being a guard then why didn't you tell the allies who you really were?" Anna asked.

Ingrid wiped her eyes. "Because I was scared to death of the Russians!" She pulled up the sleeve on her sweater to reveal the number. "I had this and it required little explanation."

"Why did you murder that woman, that kapo? You could have just beat the shit out of her." Anna asked, shrugging her shoulders.

"Because I hated myself, Anna. She was trying to imitate me and thought I would be proud of her for nearly killing a Jew. It wasn't right, but I took all my anger out on her when I wanted to split my own skull open." Ingrid replied with more vigor than intended.

Anna was silent; giving Ingrid one of those looks that once had chastised her behavior. "I could judge you, but I killed people also in the resistance before I was captured. I'm not sorry for that either. But I did what I had to do, Ingrid! The government was trying to murder me! What the hell was your excuse?"

Ingrid became defensive. "I know you think that I should have seen the reality of the situation, but I was barely eighteen when the Waffen SS approached me about posing for their recruitment posters and it got my stepfather a job. God knows he was a lazy son of a bitch. He stopped beating my mother after that and showed me off like a prized bird dog."

"I understand that we do what we have to and the propaganda was one thing, but you didn't just sit pretty for pictures. What did you do to get from a cozy studio to Auschwitz?" Anna demanded, placing the drinks and bagel sack on the ground as she slid closer to confront Ingrid.

Ingrid let out a sigh and looked down at the buttons on her sweater. "I knocked the crap out of the artist painting my portrait....I scared myself that day, Anna. You know I'd never hit anyone before, but that day a Major Richstatter was there observing and he thought my talents were better put to use elsewhere. I was sent to Ravensbrück for training, as you've probably read in the papers."

Anna studied Ingrid's quivering lips and then gazed at Agnes' headstone. "People like you caused so much pain and horror—damn it Ingrid, you were my best friend! I knew you liked the fanfare and all the Nazi bullshit, but never, NEVER did I ever imagine you would fight against me!"

Ingrid silently looked at the name *Treblinka* inscribed on the headstone. There was no going back, no amount of time or good deeds would erase her time as a Nazi camp guard. How many hundreds of people never saw her as anything but a demon in black? She pulled a small photograph from the sweater pocket. "I carried this with me everywhere, sewn inside my uniform." It was a picture of Anna as a teenager.

Awe struck Anna's face. "Why?"

"You remember that dance we had in the alley?" Anna's features softened. "I've spent my whole life wanting to feel like I did that moment when I kissed you and I never have, not even after nearly fifty years of marriage to a wonderful man. I have never felt so one with another person. I loved you so much." Ingrid's voice dwindled to a whisper. "Even though I didn't have the courage to face my feelings, the thought that you were in the world somewhere kept me from becoming a total animal.

When I found out you were at Auschwitz and close to death I was willing to do anything to make sure you lived."

Anna was dumbfounded at the admission and stared at a darkening sky where storm clouds moved in. She had been right so long ago when she feared Ingrid could not handle her emotions. What might have happened if Hitler never gained power and the Holocaust was just a horrid vision of some writer? What if they had never been apart? What sort of person would Ingrid have been then with no jack booting brutes swaying her? "You felt the same for me as I did you? Oh Ingrid, what a tragedy, what a shame….." Anna replied, tears running down her cheeks. "So you marrying a Jew wasn't just a cover?"

Ingrid shook her head. "No, not at all. I met Herschel when he was still in rabbinical school. He was a friend of the family I lived with in New York. I really cared for him, but not as much as he loved me. I wanted to be part of your world, no matter how small."

"This was not how I thought this little chat would turn out. I wanted to rip you good, to tell you no way in hell would I vouch for you in court. Go down in flames like the Nazi bitch you are!" Anna's throat tightened. "Why did you have to show me that damned picture?"

"Because next to my children and grandchildren it is the most precious thing I have. It's a little bit of frozen time when I was a naïve girl in love, you never get that back, that first kiss no matter how long you live." Ingrid smiled through tears.

Anna stared at the ground unsure of what to say or feel. What on earth would Agnes say about a camp guard sitting next to her grave? About Anna talking to her at all? Agnes would have had little sympathy for Ingrid or another woman volunteering to be an Aufseherin. She had no use for cowards who would harm others to save their own skin or feather their own nests. Jumping on the Nazi band wagon to save your own ass was no excuse. Anna had never told her partner about Ingrid, she only wanted to forget Germany and its many painful memories.

"Agnes would be furious that you bought a bench and placed it here. She would have publicized your past anywhere possible and made sure you were deported. Unlike me, Agnes did not want to forget and would not let anyone else either. Sometimes it was a pain the ass, but she saw things happening here that alarmed her and she thought a Fourth Reich was entirely possible. Remember the last time that people did nothing, she would say."

"My lawyer told me I should deny being Ingrid Brecht and it would be hard to prove otherwise. But others will come forward as I distinguished myself quite well for the SS...I only wanted you to talk about the girl you knew for the court, for what good I don't know." Ingrid appeared hopeless.

"What about all the people you've known as Ingrid Levy? Have they not come to your aid or offered any support?" Anna asked.

Ingrid chewed her lip. "I'm too ashamed to face any of them, but they have communicated with my son and daughter. Everyone thinks they must have the wrong person, the Ingrid they knew could never have been such a monster."

A roll of thunder rumbled through the clouds that twirled above them. "Where are staying?" Anna asked Ingrid as a cold rain drop splashed on her cheek.

"Nowhere, I planned on driving home after we talked. Actually, I was afraid you would not come." Ingrid grabbed up the soaked pastries and crammed them quickly into the bag.

The rhythm of rain began to crescendo as the two women got up. "Come on, we'll go to my house." Anna motioned as she ran toward her truck. "Just follow me, but park in the driveway this time!" Surprised, Ingrid grinned and jogged after Anna, tossing the trash into a bin near the gate.

The sky opened up, drenching the town and Anna could not help but feel disapproval from millions of victims who beat angry drums in the thunderheads far above with Agnes on the bass drum.

Across from the cemetery the sheriff sat in his patrol car relieved that there was no confrontation. He could not imagine being in Anna's place, but was glad to pull away and continue his rounds. Stormy nights always set a few alarms off and he would be busy enough without breaking up fights.

Nineteen

While German troops suffered in freezing cold and stole food from starving locals both in urban and rural areas just to survive, SS officers ate and drank well. The Pirates had discovered a supply route by which Nazi officers were kept fat and happy that ran through a wooded hilly area near the German/Polish border a small town used as an outpost.

Anna Mendel had many talents such as accounting, map reading and strategy that would one day aid her as a doctor, but she was also a crack shot with a rifle. She was the best sniper the Pirates had and often saved many lives by one well aimed shot at an unsuspecting Nazi.

As the war progressed it was obvious to those with any sense that the Germans were going to lose. Rather than try to ease the anger of the Allies and save what could be saved of Germany, the Nazis stepped up the murder machine in a desperate attempt to say either, "Hey world look at this great thing we are doing so why are you stopping us?" or it was a just pathetic attempt to erase evidence of the greatest mass murder in history. Anna was not sure, but things grew more lethal every day the resistance struck back.

There were times she would have done anything for a soft bed and a warm meal, but such things were rare for the Pirates as the Nazis were always searching and watching for them. Most nights were spent in holes dug into the ground in the forest, the only covers being branches placed over them for camouflage.

Food was difficult to obtain as even though they had many supporters it was very unhealthy to aid resistance fighters, or traitors as the Nazis called them. Providing eggs to such people could easily get a family member killed or a house burnt.

The Pirates refused to take provisions from local villagers and instead chose to ambush Nazi convoys bearing military rations and supplies. They wanted to pass out the booty to local people, but being caught with it would only make their existence more miserable. When an area became more infested with German troops the group would move on to the next town.

There were twenty members of Anna's group when she first joined them after escaping the work farm and only fifteen when she was captured and sent to Ravensbrück. Actually, she had allowed herself to be caught to save the others since Anna had missed a shot which had alerted Wehrmacht guards near a warehouse.

After being beaten for a week by Gestapo near Berlin, Anna was sent on to the concentration camp, Ravensbrück. Unwilling to believe that a woman had sniped so many SS officers the interrogators ignored her replies that she had been the sharp-shooter. She was only covering for her friends and the real sniper who the SS swore they would find. They chose to work her to death and draw out the suffering rather than hang her.

****

As it stormed outside and flames cracked in the fireplace Anna recalled the harsh times of her youth. She often came very close to not surviving the war; everyday was filled with anxiety and fear, w*ould this be the day she would die?*

The only light in the room was provided by the flickering flames that cast an orange glow on everything in the room including Ingrid's face as she sat in an overstuffed chair sipping coffee. Anna never thought she would see her again, much less have Ingrid sitting in her living room in Colorado.

The last hour had been filled with idle chat between the two women as they drank coffee to ward off the chill. Both had changed into sweat pants and tee shirts after being caught in the downpour. It was almost as if they were teenage girls again talking the night away about their dreams and all that was still possible; a time of innocence untainted with bad deeds and bad decisions.

"What was it like when you began training as a guard?" Anna asked slowly while staring into the fire.

"At first I had this notion that it was just a job, one I could do honorably. I was proud to be selected and thought I had a career with a government with long term plans, the thousand years Reich. It was clear right off though that we were not professionals, not just guardians of prisoners. Only those who demonstrated the right amount of authority-aggressiveness passed the program. If I had known the outcome of things I would have deliberately screwed up, but even then that was no guarantee of escape. I could have ended up an inmate much sooner." As Ingrid warmed her hands on the cup she looked to her friend and it felt like she was talking about someone else.

"Cruelty was rewarded." Anna commented.

"Yes. I have no excuses, Anna. I don't know where the coldness, meanness came from, but it was so easy to abuse that power and as bad I was there were many more violent than me. I am so ashamed of that person and wish I could separate myself from her. Ingrid Brecht died at Auschwitz."

Anna put her cup on the coffee table between them and pulled her legs up into the recliner. "I don't think that anyone really made it out of Nazi Germany the same person. I'm certainly not the woman I could have been if not for that hoodlum Hitler. It's funny that you turned to God afterwards and I told Adolf to fuck off."

"I had to believe that there was something beyond the cruel and wicked, that if you just reached out for it goodness would find you." Pain filled Ingrid's features knowing Anna had lost such a positive part of life.

"After being arrested, beaten, hunted, shipped off to the camps and finding out my family had been murdered, I came to the conclusion that either God was an asshole or that he had no power, either way the result was the same. We're on our own down here and we Jews have been chosen for nothing but abuse of the worst kind. Ever wonder why the Hebrews were the only tribe to make a contract with Yahweh? Because he was known as a hateful, selfish and cruel deity that the Sumerians and Babylonians completely avoided."

"I had no idea you knew so much about history." Ingrid replied, unsure of how to comfort her friend.

"Well, I didn't, but I wanted to know why one group of people continually got the shaft on this planet and it helped me to deal with the anger and sorrow. I needed answers and a solution where I had a choice in the matter. I chose to reject religion." Anna's attention quickly turned to the fire which snapped and crackled loudly. "Let me ask you something. How in the hell could you people eat and make merry with hundreds of people roasting not fifty yards from your table?" Her tone grew hard.

Ingrid burst into tears and covered her face, unable to speak for a time. When she controlled the crying Ingrid stared at Anna. "Okay, you want answers, you can have them! It is easy to kill and burn other beings when you convince yourself they are little more than cattle ruining your country. When you are rewarded for such behavior it is easy. When you are punished for any sign of weakness toward them it is easy. We were monsters! I survived Anna what I am supposed to do? I can't make myself drop dead!" Ingrid leaned forward and slapped the table, making the tea cups vibrate musical tones.

As the thunder rolled outside Anna got up to watch the rain from the front window. She should never have agreed to the meeting, but part of her really wanted to see Ingrid again, to get some part of her childhood back. It was a terrible mistake.

"I know what you are doing." A voice from the shadows interrupted Anna's thoughts.

Turning half way between the window and Ingrid Anna responded, "Oh you do? Please don't keep me in suspense!"

"I recognize cowardice my friend, I am an expert at it. You still care for me and do not want to. I don't blame you, but denying it won't help. I should know! " Ingrid stood up to stand next to the fire.

"Oh I'm a coward. I see and what makes you so sure I have any affection for you?" Anna made her way back to the fireplace.

"I can feel it. I still love you and I think you still love me. It isn't so strange is it? You never knew me as the black caped guard, only the stupid schoolgirl that needed you to explain the complicated world." Ingrid bit her lip and crossed her legs, waiting for a fierce backlash.

"So our lives were like a record playing on the old gramophone, some Nazi bumped into it, the needle skipped and here we are!" Anna waved her arms about like a magician.

"You're making fun of me, but in a way yes. Hitler was a deep scratch in an otherwise beautiful sonata. Do we break the whole record now because we can't hear all the notes?" Ingrid pleaded. "Can't we enjoy what we have left?"

"From what I understand, you don't have a defense for not being deported, so what are you paying the lawyer for?" Anna sat back down in her recliner. "If you're off to Germany what would we have left anyway?"

Ingrid dropped into the overstuffed chair, suddenly feeling exhausted. "He wants me to deny being Ingrid Brecht, which would be difficult to prove since the Nazis went to such trouble making me appear a Jew. Only three witnesses have come forward to claim they saw me at the camps. At my age he says can appeal long enough to let me see my grandchildren grow up. He is a Jew you know? Michael is a member of my congregation and thinks I have paid for my crimes."

"Do you?" Anna asked softly.

"I don't know what sitting in a prison cell in Berlin will do for those wanting justice. I think I have helped many hundreds of people as a rabbi's wife; I am rehabilitated if you will. I spent two years as a guard, three months as an inmate and fifty years as the best woman I could be. Yes, I think I have paid for my crimes against humanity." Ingrid frowned. "What upsets me, Anna, is that all over the world the same thing is happening and yet no one is protesting except for a few liberal groups on the web. At what point do government actions become crimes and how does one know when they go from employee to criminal?"

The doctor watched the flames silently as she finished her coffee.

"I see all these American men and women trot off to war hailed as heroes, everyone in a uniform now is held in such high regard. Do you think that anyone would resist them coming to your door and dragging off one of your relatives? No! No, there would be no resistance because the government can hurt you and ruin your life. If military men come for you then you must have done something to deserve it! If people start disappearing here who will do anything to stop it?" Ingrid shouted.

"Agnes would have, and it's kind of funny, but you two might have got along. She noticed the same things you have mentioned. Upstairs she kept a library filled with history books and anything on conspiracy theories. Agnes believed the U.S. was the Fourth Reich and has similar plans to round people up."

Anna looked to the stairs up to the right where the library still contained all of Agnes' books.

"I can see where she would have been alarmed. There are too many similarities with the here and now and 1933 Germany. It could easily happen again I'm afraid." Sadness drained Ingrid's face.

Anna smiled and slapped her knees. "Listen to us, depressing the hell out of each other on such a comfy night. There's plenty of time for digging up old bones, but no more tonight. Please stay and we'll talk in the morning. There is a quest room upstairs already made up."

Ingrid nodded at the offer and the two women turned in for the night, the flames in the fireplaces slowly went out as the rain fell.

Around two in the morning Anna woke up in a sweat with the images of skulls being ripped open by bullets, missiles that she had sent into flesh and blood brains belonging to husbands, fathers and brothers-Nazis that needed to be taken out if Germany was to be saved at all. She did what was necessary to save herself and whomever else she could. There had been no other way as the world turned its back on the Jews of Germany. Anna did not want to kill anybody, she wanted to attend medical school and heal people, something that bastard Hitler would not allow. Instead Anna and many like her were forced into fighting back to being lead off to the slaughter. She did not deserve these nightmares now.

Every sight, sound and smell from the camps invaded her sleep. The rain that usually consoled her propelled her back to days of hiding in the woods as sheets of water pounded them, forcing the resistance fighters to huddle together under tattered wool blankets and shiver in the night with growling stomachs and chilled flesh.

Anger and fear of dying steadied Anna's finger on the trigger as she dropped one German soldier or SS Officer after another. From the Axis point of view she was a war criminal-a murder and thief. If the Germans had won she would have been executed and her name trashed down through history. There would have been no reverence for the Holocaust nor would the term even been applied.

When a loud clap of thunder woke her for the second time Anna sat on the edge of the bed watching it rain through a sliding glass door that opened up onto a balcony. Jagged lightening sent flashes around the dark room making Anna feel like a little girl who needed her mother or an old doctor that wished for the warm arms of her partner.

Oh Ingrid, why did you come here?

Twenty

2006

Kansas

The next morning Eisen called his client and told her that one of the witnesses against her, Herman Weiss, had died. She now had only two women inmates claiming she was Ingrid Brecht the camp guard and Greta Hamlin who had at best only seen Brecht from a distance. He wished that she would allow him to present the denial defense as it was unlikely that Ingrid would be deported now. She was stating that she would just admit to being Brecht and go back to Germany.

Eisen had an idea of how to fight the seemingly insurmountable obstacle of the deportation requirement for anyone who had participated in Nazi war crimes. Ingrid's case was unique in that she had been a guard, but also in the end fought against the Nazi regime by freeing a prisoner and as labeled an enemy of the Nazi government.

Ingrid buttered her toast slowly after hanging up the phone wondering if she should have just lied about her past sparing her grandchildren the embarrassment of having a Nazi grandmother. How could a child ever get past that? They would not, of course. Her honesty would ultimately only make her family suffer and it had cost Herschel his life. Eisen had postponed the hearing again stating that her husband had died under the stress and she needed time to prepare her defense due to the unusual circumstances.

Anna wore a blue and white checked flannel shirt that set of her silvery hair. She read the paper at the table across from Ingrid with reading glasses that gave her the appearance of a country doctor. "Want to share?" Anna asked as she peered over the paper.

"Michael got another postponement. I can't stand the uncertainty. I just want it over, Anna. I can handle being sent back to Germany, it's my family I feel so sorry for. It's for them that I want the world to hear I am not just a beast." Ingrid put the knife down and stared at the toast unable to see any religious icons in its surface. *So much for a miracle.*

The longer they were together the more time seemed to melt away. As angry as Anna had first been upon hearing what her friend had done, as furious as she had become over Ingrid expecting her to vouch for her, Anna no longer wanted her friend sent back to Germany. She could not see what good could come of it. It would not be a popular viewpoint, especially with other survivors and they were the ones that counted with Anna. Those who had not lived through the Nazi regime had no right to judge. In her experience, the people who would criticize her the most were the ones who would look away if Muslims or gays were suddenly to be rounded up never to return.

"He thinks that the Nazis may have provided me with the best defense by calling me a Jew. It seems that they destroyed my files with the SS to completely humiliate me. Even when it was clear that the war was lost the Nazis still planned for the future." Ingrid smeared blueberry jam on her toast.

"What do your kids think? What do they want you to do?" Anna laid down the paper.

"They want me to move to Chicago and live near them and fight deportation, of course." Ingrid smiled slightly. "Do you remember the posters plastered all over Berlin pushing woman to have kids for the Fuhrer? I only had two, so I would not have had any fancy medals."

Anna laughed "Well I would have been a total disgrace since I had none; no actually I guess I was a considerate Jew and did not reproduce, so maybe ole Adolph would have been grateful if the bastard had lived." Anna thought for a moment. "You know, the attitudes of the right wingers now remind me of that same agenda then-get women to stay home and reproduce whether anyone can afford to raise children or not. Agnes would be very alarmed by the laws being passed against women now. She would be speaking out loud and clear. If we start seeing that type of propaganda on street corners maybe we need to move to Canada?"

"I didn't want a husband and children then; I wanted a career like you. I had no idea of what I wanted to do, but being strapped down at such a young age was not it. The Nazis saw little use for females, so when they thought I was great stuff I have to admit that I was proud to seen in my uniform and actually believed I had some sort of future. It's almost funny now. How very foolish we are in youth." Ingrid looked to her friend, shaking her head.

"Perhaps, but nobody knew then that the Third Reich would only last twelve years. I wouldn't have guessed it. Everyone wanted to make it through that nightmare without really knowing if maybe Nazism was the future for Germany and it was not going to end." Anna was interrupted by the phone ringing.

"Dr. Mendel."

"Anna, my sister is going into labor too early and the other doctor went to Denver. My brother-in-law is who knows where, the prick!" Cody Green was seventeen and near panic. His mother had married again to a man he hated.

"Call 911 and I'll be right there." Anna hung up and jumped up from the table. "Come with me. There are two younger children running around and I might need help."

Ingrid looked shocked. "I don't know anything about delivering babies!"

"Time to learn then." The doctor opened the kitchen door and pulled Ingrid out with her.

They took the red truck to the outside of town to a rundown trailer where three big dogs barked as the women got out. They made their way through the trash, toys and overgrown weeds to the front door held open by Cody.

He was crying. "Hurry, Mom is losing a lot of blood!"

Anna ran to the back room where Ellen Limon lay in a blood soaked bed. She looked bad and it was clear that she had miscarriaged. The youngest child, Timmy, was screaming and slapping the bed with diapers that were obviously loaded. "Cody, call the sheriff and tell him we need an escort to the hospital and get these kids outta here." Jasmine, the four year old was also crying and taking up the little room available.

Ellen could not wait for an ambulance. The cause of the miscarriage was evidenced by the black eye and bruised abdomen. "Ingrid, find me a clean sheet we can carry her out to the truck on. Ellen, I'm taking you to the hospital, just hang in there."

Ingrid stumbled around the filthy house where trash and toys were scattered everywhere. She found a flat sheet in the dryer and ran to the bedroom with it. The two women rolled the young mother onto the sheet then carried her through the path Cody had cleared for them. He held his younger siblings as his dying mother was carried passed them.

As they approached the truck the sheriff pulled up, bailed out of the patrol car, opened the tailgate for them and jumped up in the bed to pull Ellen into it. "There was a pile up the freeway, so we'll probably get her there faster." He stated, breathing heavily.

Ellen had passed out when Anna stepped into the bed. "We need to get a move on or she won't make it." The doctor said in a low tone so the three children approaching the truck would not hear. "Ingrid, you drive my truck and follow the sheriff."

An old beat up pickup barreled down the street toward them, running through the rickety fence then slamming on the brakes behind the patrol car. Kyle Limon jumped out of his truck waving a shotgun around. "Goddamn it! What is that dyke doing with my wife?"

Climbing over the side of the pickup bed the sheriff pulled his 9mm out the holster. Kyle was drunk and pissed, but not as out of control as he'd seen in the past. There was still a chance to talk him down. "Kyle, Ellen has miscarriaged and bleeding out. If we don't get her to the doctor she will die."

Kyle studied the other woman standing near the truck as Anna also left the bed. "Who the fuck is that? Oh shit, no, no, no! That Nazi bitch ain't even in my yard! Christ almighty."

"Jesus, Kyle! We're talking life and death here! Get outta the way and let us help Ellen." Sheriff Beecher shouted. His eyes widen when Limon pointed the gun at Anna.

"Why'd you bring that Nazi slut here you fucking dyke? Get away from my wife!" Kyle took a step toward the two women.

"Drop the damned gun Limon. I will not tell you again." Beecher shouted.

"Kids, get back in the house!" Anna commanded, which seemed anger Limon more.

When he brought the shotgun up to his shoulder level with the doctor's face Ingrid shoved Anna hard to the ground, catching the shot in the middle of her back. The terrified children ran back into the house, shutting the door on their father.

Beecher put a slug in Limon's forehead before Kyle could move toward the house. A bemused look played over his features as the drunk dropped to his knees and then finally onto his face smashing a beer can. The sheriff ran to the car radio and demanded a chopper. "Get it here now, damn it!"

Ingrid lay on the ground stunned, her eyes staring at the clouds above and not blinking. Anna crawled over to her to check vital and neurological signs. She could not move her legs. "You'll be okay, Ingrid.

Cody brought out blankets for his mother and the wounded stranger. "Here, they might go into shock." The boy wanted to be a paramedic, so he studied emergency medicine when he had the time.

The patrol car radio announced that a chopper was ten minutes away. "10-4." Beecher responded not at all sure it would be fast enough for either victim.

"I should never have asked her to come." Anna fought tears.

"No now, I would have done the same. You had no idea what this sack of shit was going to do or whether he'd even be back here. Hell, he usually drives on down to that whore of his." Beecher climbed into the back of Anna's truck with Cody to wrap the blanket around Ellen. Her pulse was weak, but steady.

All of a sudden Ingrid began to sing *Edelweiss*, shocking those around her. "Sometimes people with spinal trauma will sing or cry." Anna explained as Ingrid sang with her eyes shining. It was not a good sign along with the fact that Ingrid could not feel her legs.

The chopper soon hovered over them as the pilot decided to land in the intersection. The paramedics quickly unloaded a gurney and maneuvered it through the yard's obstacle course. The man and woman were surprised to see two patients. There was only room for one as the chopper had already picked up an accident victim.

"Take Ellen, we'll wait for the ambulance on Ingrid." Anna ordered the paramedics while pointing to the truck. "She's lost a great deal of blood."

"We'll take good care of her, Doc and we'll check on that ambulance in the air." Kate Sears replied as they transferred Ellen to the gurney. She grinned as Ingrid sang about blossoms of snow. "Last time I heard a patient sing at a scene it was about having friends in low places."

As the chopper lifted up past the trees the blades threw lawn chairs, milk cartons and dirt everywhere. Anna drew the blanket up over Ingrid's face. She heard Beecher calling for back up to secure the crime scene and for social services to take the children until Ellen's family could arrive from Alabama.

Anna rode with Ingrid when the ambulance came. She would be taken to the trauma center in Denver where Ellen had flown. The paramedics were good, so Anna let them do their jobs and acted as a friend rather than a doctor. Ingrid seemed to be in no serious pain, but did complain about the stinging in her lower back.

She thought about the hurtful remarks the wife beater had tossed at them. Sadly, there would be people who believed that he was right in not wanting a "dyke and Nazi" around his wife. The fact that he deliberately aborted the baby would mean little since he still had a "traditional" family. Abusing them was a man's right, so was drinking up the rent and grocery money.

For the second time Ingrid the Nazi had saved Anna's life and she would not abandon her old friend now. The doctor greatly feared that Ingrid would be paralyzed from the waist down. At age eighty-five she would not recover quickly.

A Denver reporter noising around the Rocky Mountain Regional Trauma Center discovered the identity of the gunshot victim flown in from the small town of Wellsprings. He promptly wrote a piece for the Denver Post morning edition that hit the streets while Ingrid was in surgical ICU.

Once again Ingrid Levy/Brecht was back in the spotlight, but this time her husband's former congregation in Chicago made an unexpected statement while she was still in the surgical intensive care.

"We ask that the world allow this woman, whom we only know as Ingrid Levy, to be at peace while she recovers and to examine the life she has lead since coming to this country. We are traditionally a land of second chances and to be frank, the U.S. government let thousands of former Nazis immigrate and live out their lives here in exchange for information. No one seems to be concerned about that issue.

Ingrid Levy has accomplished many good things upon arriving here. Surely a woman who raised several million dollars for a hospital burn unit deserves the same chance as the Nazi scientist who invented rockets used against Americans? Von Braun was never asked to leave."

The hospital prepared for major trouble from both sides of the questions as to whether the old woman should stay or go. Most people did not appear to be concerned with acts committed before many were even born. Security tossed out a few neo-Nazis and some from the other end of the spectrum who wanted Ingrid shipped out right then, but worries of the modern world pulled attention to unpaid mortgages, unemployment and school violence. An eighty-five year old woman with fifty year old crimes fed a brief rise of interest then fell just as quickly.

Twenty-One

2006

Colorado

Anna Mendel waited for three hours during Ingrid's procedure. The surgery had gone well with the shotgun pellets missing her spinal cord, but doing internal damage by nicking a kidney and perforating the bowl.

She had met Ingrid's children, David and Sarah who were polar opposites. The son was medium height, dark haired and browned eyed like his father and Sarah tall and blonde like her mother. Both clearly cared for their mother, but David was more resentful of her betrayal and secrecy. The emotional struggle was more evident in him than his sister.

They approached down the hall to the waiting room with three cups of coffee-one for Anna as well. The siblings were solemn as if some heated conversation had preceded buying the equally hot beverages. Anna didn't envy their positions as she had a difficult enough time with Ingrid just being a friend let alone her mother. The three of them sat sipping coffee for thirty minutes when a nurse entered the room looking for family of Ingrid Levy.

She was awake and able to move her legs, which was an enormous relief, in spite of David's remark that a wheelchair might have made his mother more sympathetic for the media. Sarah threw him a disapproving glance and nodded for the nurse to continue. Ingrid could have two visitors at a time every two hours.

David told Sarah and Anna to go first, that he had to find a bathroom. The two women shrugged it off and tossed their empty cups into a trash can near the waiting room door.

Ingrid was groggy, but aware that her daughter and friend stood near the bed. She smiled amid the machines and tubes. "I feel like a pin cushion."

"Oh, it's not so bad now. You should have seen yourself right after surgery. Are you feeling any pain?" Anna asked, the doctor in her always leading the way.

The patient shook her head. "No, whatever they are giving me is very good. Are you okay?" Ingrid asked Anna.

"Yes, thanks to you playing the hero! The kids are safe, but the cops had to shoot Kyle. At least he won't be beating on them anymore." Anna replied as she glanced David standing at the door.

"I can't imagine how the state could turn a blind eye to his behavior and not protect those children from him...." Ingrid pushed the button to raise the bed slightly.

David stepped into the room, his lip quivering. "Look who's talking! Maybe I should keep my kids away from you, mother? Cause I don't really know you or what you're capable of!" Anger and pain moistened his eyes as he approached the bed where his shocked mother stared at him wide-eyed.

Sarah shoved her brother. "What the hell, she just got out of major surgery!"

"Like you haven't thought it? Come on, Sarah. Tell me it doesn't bother you that Mom here was a goose stepping Nazi?" David pointed at Ingrid.

"He has a right to be mad. I lied to all of you for years." Ingrid's voice was strained and the stress made her abdominal muscles tense up and her pulse increase.

The raised voices brought the charge nurse running to intervene. The RN, an intense older woman with years of experience instantly commanded the situation. "I have to ask that you leave now. This patient is still critically ill."

"Of course, we'll let her rest and come back later." Anna glared at David. "Some of us will come back later."

David Levy reacted like a spoiled five year old, which didn't really surprise Anna since she knew Ingrid had indulged her children their entire lives, leaving them wanting or needing nothing. He took it only as an affront to himself that his mother didn't consider his future when she signed on the dotted line.

"I'm not some fine piece of china. Nobody needs to walk on egg shells around me." Ingrid protested as the nurse increased the morphine drip.

"You're my patient dear; let me take care of you. You have a lot of healing to do and need rest." The RN waved a finger at Ingrid. "There will be plenty of time later for family talks."

Sarah pushed her brother out the door, her features firmly set. He flashed an indignant expression while being ushered through the door. Anna threw Ingrid a reassuring smile, but could tell David's remark had cut her good. She appeared defeated as sleep overcame her.

Once in the hall Anna put a finger to her lips to warn the siblings about any arguing within earshot. The three of them walked briskly down the corridor to the elevator.

"How could you?" Sarah demanded of her brother who by now was defensive. "It could have waited!"

He ground his teeth for a moment. "She brought it on by judging that guy. How is she any different?"

Anna stood close to the taller man. "Ingrid has been nothing but good to you. You have not earned the right to judge her past as I have. You never knew Ingrid Brecht because she did not want you too! You should be ashamed of yourself."

"Oh, so you think that it shouldn't hurt to know that your mother was a camp guard, something that you have heard nothing but negative shit about your whole life? Forgive me if I can't just swallow the fact that my mother was a mean bitch that cared nothing for anybody under her!" David glared at the short doctor still standing close. "Some of us take it better than others." He looked to his sister.

"I'm not perfect, David. Of course it bothers me, and I do feel betrayed, but what should be the right response? As Anna says, we have never known the woman she was in Germany. Our children only know a kind, generous grandmother. She can't rewind the past, David." Sarah's shoulders dropped. "Would you rather she'd have died?"

"I don't know, Sarah. We're never going to get past this mess and you know it. Our kids will always be the kids with the

Nazi grandma. I don't see how this will ever turn out good." He suddenly appeared tired as the anger ebbed.

"Let's just get her healed up and then deal with hostile feelings. The fact is Ingrid didn't die and you will have to face her." Anna watched the elevator light turn green and the doors open onto the hospital lobby. "I'm going to grab something to eat. Wanna go with me?" The brother and sister looked to each other like they had just had a fight in the backyard, but nodded their heads. "We'll take my car."

Twenty-Two

2006

Kansas

Michael Eisen didn't wish any harm on his client, but getting shot while saving the same friend she had saved at Auschwitz was good publicity. In reality he had no legal recourse to keep Ingrid from being deported. Time and appeals were all he had to keep her in the United States. Other Nazi war criminals had denied being the offending individuals and had bought a great deal of time, but Ingrid just admitted she was the guard, Ingrid Brecht. Eisen had nothing to build a defense on. Now at least he could postpone the hearing.

He wasn't sure how to feel about former Nazis anymore. The U.S. thought nothing of letting thousands of them enter the country that had hurt many more people than camp guards under Operation Paperclip. As long as they had some skill the government wanted to use against the dreaded Soviets they got houses, careers and freedom in America. How did that make it right?

Even when Ingrid finally ran out of appeals it was no guarantee that Germany would accept her back, and then she would be without a country and citizenship. Germany had taken some major war criminals back for trial that had well documented cases of personally being involved as camp directors or officers with real power. If deported back to her homeland, Ingrid would be arrested at the airport and taken to jail in Berlin where she had last lived to await trial.

He believed that people needed to pay for their crimes, but struggled with Ingrid's situation which as far as Eisen knew was unique. Eisen also wondered if his own children would do the same as she had when faced with no future outside the regime at hand. In the end Ingrid had turned back to the light and remained there. What was the purpose in dragging an old woman into a foreign jail cell to die? She was fully aware that she had done wrong and did everything possible to make up for it. Ingrid had rehabilitated herself wasn't that the goal?

Ingrid's injuries were ones that could cause ongoing problems. There was a pellet fragment near her spinal cord too close to risk removing it. She was far from being out of the woods. If the piece of metal moved Ingrid would not have to worry about Germany anymore.

Twenty-Three

2006

Colorado

Anna Mendel sat on her porch swing allowing tears to flow the sun went down. After several days at the hospital she had come home to wash clothes and rest a bit. While throwing shirts and jeans into the dryer the door bell rang.

It was four members of Agnes' activist group, *From the Ashes.* They worked to prevent any possibility of a repeat of Nazi Germany in the United States. The group monitored changes to laws and attitudes that might harm the spirit of freedom in America and they had no tolerance for Anna's compassion for a former Nazi.

The two women and a man were Holocaust survivors and relatives of victims, good people who were aghast at Anna's alliance with Ingrid Brecht and challenged her wisdom regarding the friendship for over an hour. Agnes would be appalled, they said. How could she stand by such a woman?

Anna found the words coming out of her mouth nearly impudent against the sound arguments of Agnes' friends. Would she be ashamed of Anna actions? The doctor had doubts now, felt defensive and lashed back at the verbal beating.

They had no understanding of what it had been like to lay in that filthy, flea infected bed, wounded, an eye gashed out, praying for death rather than face any more pain and humiliation and then be enveloped in those warm arms. Barely conscious, the scent of a familiar perfume had filled the air as Anna's nose pressed against dry cleaned wool, the woman rocking her and weeping in that pig sty. At the time it seemed as though God had finally quit ignoring the terror and sent an angel to pluck at least one soul from hell.

It was not a feeling easily described and not one Anna felt she should have to justify. Because of Ingrid Anna became a doctor and had lived a long life. She was now returning the favor.

"I doubt very much that Agnes is displeased with me, if she were I also have no doubt that she would let me know about it! Ingrid thinks the very same way as you all. She watches the news and is very concerned that the same thing could happen here, that young people could buy into the bullshit like she did. Nobody knows any better than Ingrid that there comes a point of no return and you must live with your choices and hope you do not drown in them. Please leave me alone. I don't owe you anything. I paid my damned dues!"

Her visitors appeared surprised at Anna's reaction; as if they thought a lecture would simply turn her around. Their tones softened as they apologized for attacking her.

"I understand your mission; just don't tell me what to do or how to do it. I have no use for Nazis or those that glorify them. I am helping one childhood friend that saved me from a disgusting death-period. Don't make anything political out of it." Anna's eyes burned like coals.

Angel Goodman listened as Anna spoke. She had been at Treblinka like Agnes. "We don't mean to be cruel Anna, please do not take it that way. We only fear that if you bring sympathy to Ingrid's plight people will think that former Nazis are not worth prosecuting and people will just forget. Forgetting allows evil to repeat."

"It looks like your supporting a Nazi." Karl Nussman's tone was accusing. The son of a Jewish doctor killed at Sachshausen, he was angry at Anna.

"If you were not Jewish in Germany, who the hell was not a Nazi? Hm? Life was much easier if you were a party member; you had no future if you were not. You own a bar, don't you Karl? If not for a bunch of unemployed drunks Hitler would have had no audience to spew his crap on. I mean, if we're going to point fingers at who could encourage right wing horseshit let's be honest!" Dr. Mendel shouted back at him.

"What do the town people think of your association with her?" Kristen Parker asked softly, her white hair tossed about gently by the ceiling fan.

"Some aren't happy about it, others understand and others don't give a damn. I'm retired, so I don't worry about lost business anymore." Anna finished the beer she was drinking and crushed the can. "Ingrid's more Jewish than I am and shot up. For God's sake leave her and me alone."

"I'm trying to understand Anna. You and Agnes have always been my favorite people in the group. I was in a cattle car to Auschwitz that was so crammed full we could barely move. No food, no water and one waste bucket for over a hundred people. I remember very well the guards who pulled us off the train then sorted us out for the slaughter, for all I know Ingrid was one of them who decided my sick mother and little brother should be gassed and burnt. Why Anna?" Parker's throat tightened.

Anna studied the crumpled can in her hand. "You think that I don't struggle daily with this? All I can tell you is that Ingrid took up for me when it was against her best interest to do so and got me released from that hell, and then she caught bullets for me and once again I am still breathing because of her. I have loved few people in this life as my heart is so cautious, but it has no fear of Ingrid."

"That may be all well for you, but many will think that if a Holocaust survivor can blow off a camp guard's past then it must not be that bad." Karl growled at her.

"You want me to abandon a friend who made a bad choice many years ago, one who felt like she had no choice, one who has only tried to bury that past with good deeds. No, I can't do that. I won't do that. " Anna stood up.

Kristen and Angela followed suit, with Karl getting up slowly after a few seconds. The four people studied each other almost mournfully. Neither side has convinced the other to change viewpoints.

"You are always welcome to the group, Anna. I don't really understand your situation, but I had friends in Germany too, ones that belonged to the Hitler Youth. I never saw them again after being deported, but I don't know what I would do now if I should meet them." Angela stated.

"Ingrid is a little snapshot of a childhood stolen from me by a ridiculous troll that wrecked our country. I lost my family long ago and I need this tiny bit of my past. The Ingrid I loved then and the one in the hospital is not the Ingrid the witnesses knew, the one who was a guard for less than two years six decades ago. I can't explain it any better than that. It may seem pathetic, but the sun shone on my early life so briefly that I want to keep what little I can."

After the three left Anna went outside and cried as if her heart were sinking along with the sun behind the trees.

Twenty-Four

One year later

Germany had no interest in prosecuting Ingrid Levy and refused to accept her for deportation. A guard who had turned against the Nazis and paid the price for it was not worth the time or expense of a trial the government was not sure it would win. The economy in Germany was not better than in the states were courts were only running four days a week.

A year after Ingrid's discharge from the hospital Eisen called her in Chicago with the news. After staying with Anna for two months convalescing Ingrid had moved in with her daughter in Illinois. The news should have been good to hear, but Ingrid was a pariah.

The people of Wellsprings, Colorado were not happy that the former camp guard was living in their town and ostracized Anna. Ingrid left to avoid ruining Anna's life. The final straw was when bright red swastikas were painted on Anna's garage doors.

Things were not going well in Chicago either, while there were people who supported Ingrid it was not politically correct to make it known. She well understood the lack of courage to buck the system. Ingrid had not had the backbone to turn down the SS job or infuriate her stepfather.

It pained her to see her grandchildren come home crying or hear people saying that there was no way her late husband could not have known Ingrid's real identity. The general attitude was that the rotten fruit didn't fall far from the tree.

She may as well have been tried and found guilty as the outcome was the same. Where could Ingrid go where she would not be hated? The stress on Sarah and David's marriages was clear and Ingrid knew she could not remain near them. The only way for her family to recover was for Ingrid to disappear-out of sight out of mind.

Anna called her often, worried about what kind of life Ingrid had now. She had not asked Ingrid to leave Colorado as Anna felt her friends were her own damned business, especially after over thirty years of being the town doctor. She was considering selling her house and leaving the area. Nothing would ever be the same and as stubborn as Anna Mendel was, getting the cold shoulder grocery shopping or gassing up was becoming intolerable.

One cold rainy afternoon Anna arrived at Sarah's house outside Chicago and was told Ingrid had left to some undisclosed location. David had blown up at his mother again two days earlier shouting the cruelest of remarks and then Ingrid's room was cleared of her belongings. She left a brief note stating that the best thing she could do for her family was to leave and perhaps their lives could one day return to normal.

Ingrid was sitting at the John F. Kennedy International Airport in New York as Anna was gazing around her empty room in Chicago. She carried a one-way ticket to Berlin. Anna had left numerous messages on her cell phones as had Sarah, but Ingrid would not tell them where she was until back in Germany.

It was clear that nothing she could ever do would erase the past. She would never be anything but a Nazi bitch to the world. What she would do in Berlin was a mystery as it was a new city reborn after the war. When her flight was announced Ingrid Levy picked up her suitcase and boarded the plane for a country that had been ravaged when she left it as younger woman. Never had she dreamed that years later she would return to Germany as a refugee from a different kind of war.

A young couple with a small child sat across the aisle from her. They spoke German to the boy who could go easily from German to English. Ingrid had not wanted her children to speak German at home and thus never used it with Sarah and David. It was not a part of her life she wished to share with them, but it touched her to see people proud of their heritage and a younger generation that would be familiar with the new Germany.

When Ingrid nodded off two hours later she had nightmares of her training days at Ravensbrück. The images were crystal clear, the sights, sounds and smells of the camp vivid. It was as if Ingrid had stepped into a time machine. In the dream though she had seen the cruelty expected of the guards and had deliberately flunked out of the program. She returned home to her stepfather's rage and was thrown into the street during a thunderstorm where she spent the night huddled under a tree in the Tiergarten, cold and wounded but innocent of any wrong doing.

A stewardess passing out dinner from a silver cart woke her up to the twenty-first century and the flight to Berlin. She felt a hellish headache burn through her brain and declined the tray, opting instead for a Lortab from her purse. Nearly half way to Germany she called her daughter.

Sarah was hurt and angry at her mother's decision to abandon them as she described it. Ingrid didn't see it that way she explained. How could Sarah and her young family ever have a normal life with Ingrid around? David was right. It was better for everyone if she just left and eventually the media would move on to other topics.

An emotional Sarah countered with the fact that they were family and should stick together. Ingrid agreed in any other situation, but most people did not have Nazi camp guards as grandmothers. It would be better this way and there was always email, videos and chat. Ingrid would not really be separated from her family, just out of sight to everybody else in their world. For six months, then come home, Sarah relented and Ingrid agreed with no intention of returning to Chicago. She also called David and left a message on his answering machine knowing that he was standing there listening to her.

He had always been more sensitive and self-centered than his sister and took Ingrid's betrayal as a personal assault. Deep down David knew his mother was not the Ingrid Brecht in the news, but he was feeling pressure at work from veterans of various wars. A talented chemical engineer, David would not be fired, but the atmosphere at the plant had definitely changed. His kids were not catching that much slack because younger generations barely knew what a Nazi was or didn't understand the uproar. David didn't appreciate being treated like a pervert who had to be a closet neo-Nazi.

The next call was to Anna who was home in Colorado after not being able to locate her old friend. The doctor was flabbergasted that Ingrid was going back to Germany. Why, she asked. Germany didn't want her for crimes and the U.S. couldn't prosecute her for war crimes. Ingrid retorted that her American citizenship would eventually be revoked, so what did it matter?

Anna finally got an address out Ingrid for an apartment near the Tiergarten. She rented it for a month until further plans could be made. As far as German authorities were concerned Ingrid was just a tourist. The apartment at 24 Einemstrasse was fully furnished including dishes, which was perfect for a woman who had left with two suitcases.

"Are you insane?" Anna demanded.

"I just need to do this, okay? There are no long term plans, please, let me figure things out on my own." Ingrid pleaded.

"I'm worried about you, Ingrid. What the hell could you figure out in modern Berlin? It's a whole new city. You may as well head to Moscow for all the difference it will make!" Anna argued with strain in her voice. Ingrid knew no one in Germany. "Does Eisen know what you're doing? I'm surprised that you were even allowed to leave the country."

"I'll be fine, Anna and I'm sure that if I had bought a ticket for Argentina they would have stopped me. As things are, they don't give a shit if I go back to Germany. I did tell Michael that I was going back voluntarily. He thought I was nuts too, but contacted immigration and told them where I was going." The couple across the aisle seemed amazed to hear an old lady swear, bringing a slight grin to her lips. If using dirty words was her biggest problem Ingrid would be delighted. "I won't be able to go back home, Anna. This is a one way trip."

"I don't understand why Germany allowed you to come back, Ingrid. The Nazis gave Germany two deep black eyes and they're sensitive about it." Dr. Mendel questioned.

"True, but there are also movements pushing for those who refused to follow orders to be recognized. Of course, most are trying to vindicate their fathers and grandfathers who were in the regular army and not SS units, but I do have supporters who are not neo-Nazis. I won't be completely alone." Ingrid offered.

Anna didn't buy it. The movement Ingrid referred to was a response to an exhibit in various German cities such a Munich and Berlin that exposed the collaboration of German soldiers in the oppression and killing of Jews. Many did not want to accept the fact that ordinary soldiers who were expected to protect people stood around and watched people being abused or were actively involved. The old excuse, *I was just following orders* was being challenged and it did not help Ingrid's case that many soldiers that refused to obey orders suffered no consequences for their actions.

"I wish you had talked to me first." Anna said firmly.

"And you know why I didn't! You and my daughter would have tried to stop me; my son is a different story. I'm sure David will be glad to me gone." Ingrid's voice quivered.

"Ingrid, you know he is just hurt and angry. I doubt very much he wants his mother in another country." Anna tried to comfort her friend, but she heard David's tone at the hospital and wondered if Ingrid wasn't right.

"I think we need some space from each other. If they want to come visit later I will send my address. Let things die down a bit first." Ingrid smiled as a stewardess offered her a small bottle of Grey Goose vodka.

Anna reflected a moment on Ingrid, the friend who could no longer go home and didn't really belong where she was going. "Well, you're somewhere over the Atlantic Ocean, so you've won the argument. Call me when you land in Berlin."

"I will. Don't worry I can land on my feet. I've done it before-we've both done it before."

Twenty-Five

2007

Germany

Berlin was a new city vastly different from the one she left as a young woman. It was fresh and modern with monuments to the Holocaust everywhere. The Tiergarten had been rebuilt as after the war freezing residents had chopped down the old trees for firewood and the animals in the zoo were scattered or perhaps even roasted. The new park was beautiful and full of life.

The old building where Ingrid had lived with her parents and brother, Albert, had been so renovated that she did not recognize it. There was little in 2006 that resembled the Berlin of 1940 in that the atmosphere was free and light, the oppression and stress of the Nazi era cured like an infectious disease. It was like tossing a fiery skillet into a snow bank.

Her apartment at Einem Place was nicely decorated with three bedrooms and two baths. Ingrid planned for her family to visit and so rented the larger flat. It came with a television with both national and international channels so she still would be connected with American shows. She bought a laptop that was compatible with the 220 electrical sockets in Germany for emailing and Facebook use.

Ingrid's favorite place was still the Tiergarten where she and Anna used to ride their bicycles. Though it had changed much through the nearly two hundred years since it was created, the park was still a refuge from urban life. The ponds, woods, streams and open fields spoke of country life, and for a time, city dwellers could experience rural peace and quiet. A quick ride on the train to the Berlin-Tiergarten Station brought her to the park where cyclists were still attracted to the many forested paths, bringing a youthful spark to Ingrid's aging heart.

One addition that Ingrid found disturbing was the memorial built between 2003 and 2005, the *Memorial to Murdered Jews of Europe*. It was a gray concrete monstrosity that was supposed to honor fallen victims. The fact that a company that had made Zyklon B gas used in the gas chambers was involved should have been an omen to the city. It brought no comfort to Ingrid as it reminded her of the cold, harsh, drab reality of Nazi Germany. If anything, it made her feel that a Nazi hand could reach out and pull her back into the abyss if she came too near the 2711 erect cement slabs. It scared the hell out of Ingrid who never went back to that area of the park.

As the weeks passed Ingrid began to feel isolated and hopeless, though she never let her family or Anna know. She even heard from members of Herschel's congregation in Chicago who asked if she needed anything. What Ingrid needed was her life back, which was not going to happen.

She had not attempted to attend services at any synagogue in Berlin, feeling as if those inside could see a swastika engraved in her forehead in spite of the Auschwitz camp number on her arm. There was too great a chance that someone would recognize her and cause a scene. Ingrid had no desire to inflict anymore grief on people or herself for that matter.

Eisen had managed to allow Ingrid to continue to draw her husband's social security after a six month battle as in the end the judge decided Rabbi Levy's contributions were valid and his wife could receive checks based on his contributions. The legality of their marriage was another issue if the Feds wanted to pursue it. So, she could easily not have an income except for the $20,000 in savings, an amount that would not last long in the current economy.

Being in Berlin and hearing spoken German poked holes in time's healing fabric for Ingrid who felt the old Ingrid Brecht climbing through the jagged tears. Dreams of pre-war Berlin became clearer helping her to recall how the city used to look when boring schoolwork was her main problem aside from a drunken stepfather. The smells of her mother's cooking were so vivid Ingrid was crestfallen to awaken to an empty sterile apartment.

She was caught between two worlds with every stroll down the busy streets. A small café was inserted where the Mendel shop used to be, appearing nothing as it did when she would meet her best friend there. The red brick and natural wood exterior was painted a glossy white with green trim. Customers sipping espresso sat near the large front window watching passing traffic or engulfed in conversation.

Bicycles and pedestrians still speckled the streets and sidewalks, but there were many more cars now and the noise level much higher than Ingrid remembered. No hope of seeing a familiar friendly face in the crowds wore on her as did returning home alone every day. Emails and messaging were not filling the void.

One day after watching parents and grandparents interacting with children at the zoo Ingrid came home to a hot bath for her aching back and cried until she could shed no more tears. She just wanted to die.

Twenty-Six

2007

Berlin, Germany

Ingrid stopped answering her phone or email for two days striking terror in her daughter, Sarah who called Dr. Mendel. Anna too was worried about Ingrid's state of mind. How could anyone handle her predicament and not be damaged mentally and emotionally? Secluding herself was not a good sign.

The nervous doctor booked a flight to Berlin on Air France for almost $1800. Highway robbery Anna mumbled to herself after buying the tickets online. There was one seat left with stopovers in Atlanta and Paris, France. She quickly packed and drove to the Denver airport as the flight left in three hours. In thirty-two hours Anna would return to Germany and the city she once called home.

It was beginning to sprinkle when Dr. Mendel arrived at Ingrid's apartment to find no one home. She knocked on the manager's door and a middle-aged woman answered.

"Hello, I'm Dr. Anna Mendel. I'm here to see my friend Ingrid Levy. Do you know where she might be?" Anna inquired hopefully.

Greta Berger finished chewing a bite of sandwich and wiped her mouth off. "You're the first visitor she'd had. Frau Levy spends a lot of time in the Tiergarten, but I hardly think she's there now with the rain and all."

"Do you have a piece of paper so I could leave a note on her door?" The doctor asked losing patience with the woman who took another bite and studied Anna like she was the next course.

The woman shrugged and handed Anna a note pad and pen. "You called her? Ingrid's got a cell phone."

Anna peered at Berger over the tops of her glasses. "Indeed, but she is not answering it and I'm a bit concerned."

"She does seem somewhat down. Would you like to check things out just to be sure, I mean she is elderly." Greta finally put the sandwich on the counter and reached for the master key.

"Yes, if that would be okay. As you say, both of us are elderly." Anna smiled.

The apartment was dark and silent until Anna flipped the light switch. It was clearly not Ingrid's choice of décor, but an impersonal comfortable. Her laptop was off and the cell phone lay on the table next to it. The bed was left unmade with no sign of Ingrid.

"You say she likes the Tiergarten? Any particular part?" Anna asked as she noticed the shower stall was dry.

"She doesn't exactly confide in me, but I have heard her on the phone talking about the Holocaust memorial. Didn't sound like it was a favorite spot though." Greta responded with a flat tone.

"Thank you for your help." Anna headed for the front door, prompting the manager to follow. "You wouldn't have a train schedule would you?"

Berger nodded. "Yes, there is a shelf in the corridor with some maps and pamphlets. Many of our residents are tourists or temporary workers."

Anna grabbed a train and bus schedule and a Berlin map and rushed out into the rain. The 100 bus took her up the middle of the Tiergarten where she got off near Neuer See, a large lake south of the Lowenbrucke (Lionsbridge). When the two women were girls they would spend time in the wooded areas to avoid being seen together, though Anna often hid the yellow star she was forced to wear. It was till dangerous for Aryans to fraternize with Jews.

The Tiergarten was full of wild areas with creeks and isolated paths where people could hide for a time from urban life. After the war the park was a wasteland completely unrecognizable and Anna was pleased to see if come back to life.

The manager had stated hearing Ingrid talk about the memorial to Jews, but if she didn't like it Anna doubted Ingrid would be there now. More than likely she was sitting on a bench somewhere with few people around and near water.

Anna walked for forty-five minutes before turning onto a path off of Grosser Weg south of the Lionsbridge. Thunder cracked above releasing more rain onto those now running with no umbrellas. The doctor had bought a small one from a vender that offered some protection against chilly raindrops, but little when the wind picked up.

When she approached the stream south of the bridge Anna spotted Ingrid sitting on a bench near the water, her arms crossed tightly against the cold. Strolling slowly Anna stopped near the bench until Ingrid noticed her. At first Ingrid looked puzzled until she realized the stranger was her friend.

****

After nearly three weeks alone Ingrid suffered from severe depression. She was in limbo and belonged nowhere with no citizenship in the United States or Germany. There wasn't any point to her continued life with nothing to look forward to besides television, emails and phone calls. The cold emptiness of the apartment was becoming intolerable.

Being anywhere was better than rotting in that apartment so Ingrid spent most of her time in the Tiergarten and in spite of the fact that she hated the Memorial to the Murdered Jews of Europe, Ingrid found herself drawn back to it and eventually she decided to kill herself after staring at the 2711 waving slabs that screamed at her. She would overdose on the pain killers still prescribed for her back injury.

It was not storming that morning when she caught the S-bahn to the park, but when near the Lionsbridge it began to sprinkle sending many patrons scrambling for cover. She sat down on a bench near the stream and let the rain soak her through. Maybe God wanted to her catch pneumonia and die, the last decades of good works swept under the rug and not entered into any heavenly log.

After awhile in the chilly rain Ingrid felt numb and was resigned to ending her life when she returned to that tomb of a dwelling. She watched the stream bubble as it was pounded by huge raindrops, much like the park had when bombed by the Allies so many years ago. She would never be paid up.

A figure appeared to her left, making Ingrid jerk with surprise. What other fool was out in a storm?

****

"What the hell are you doing?" The doctor feigned anger. Mist rose from the warm water giving the trees a hazy appearance. Anna rushed to the bench and hugged Ingrid who held her tight.

Ingrid chuckled. "Do you know what this place is known for?"

"We used to come here and play in the water. So what is it known for now?" Anna pulled back raising her eyebrows.

"A cruising spot for gays." She laughed.

Anna shook her head. "No shit. I guess it was prophetical for me, Ja?"

"How did you find me?" Ingrid pulled her friend back into her arms, partly in affection and also to ward off the chill deep in her bones.

"Your rather oddball landlady. So why have you been avoiding us all?" Anna looked at her friend's face and saw the strain in her eyes. They held the umbrella together as it rained harder.

"I've been having a hard time of it. I don't know what to say to anyone and I don't want to depress anybody with my negative thoughts." Ingrid looked again to the raindrops plopping in the stream.

"You can tell me anything. Don't be afraid of bumming me out." Anna reassured her.

"I've thought of suicide, Anna. I feel so worthless and alone...." Ingrid broke down, laying her head on Anna's shoulder.

"Do you remember us clinging together here as young girls, daring the Nazis to break us up?" Anna's voice cracked as thunder rolled. Ingrid nodded silently.

Then the Strasse 17 Juni that now bisects the park was called the East-West Axis and Hitler had lined the wide boulevard with hundreds of red, black and white flags with swastikas. The Tiergarten, the Garden of the Beasts, provided a temporary refuge for them from beasts rooting their way through a once proud city.

Anna looked down at Ingrid's face which seemed youthful in the soft light as if time had not passed, and while the Nazis were in power, most of the horrors that would occur were still in the future and might still be prevented.

Anna kissed her friend's forehead. "I've had my heart broken twice in this life. Once when the Nazis killed my family and again when Agnes died. If you hurt yourself that would make a third, please don't do that to me and yes, I'm being selfish! I don't care what you did in the camps as no matter how bad you might have been, you still managed to reach through the slime and pull me out of it. I've made a few enemies standing up for you, but that is what friends do, Ingrid."

"I was horrified to see what that kapo had done to you, it made my heart bleed and it was as if I woke up suddenly from a nightmare and tried to wipe that Nazi grime from my body."

Ingrid responded as the rain ran down her face and soaked her clothes unshielded by the umbrella. She looked up at Anna.

"When I found myself wrapped in those warm arms I knew deep down it was you. Oh, I was too sick to respond, but I recalled the dance in the alley and the way you held me tight and kissed me and I knew it was you in that camp! I imagined you were still holding me tight in Berlin and nothing could ever hurt me again." Anna began to cry. "I love you, Ingrid. Let's share what little time we have left with each other and put this nightmare behind us."

Ingrid straightened up and kissed Anna as she had decades ago, letting the umbrella fall to the ground as the thunder drummed in the clouds. "Oh Anna, I've caused so much pain. My husband Herschel died from the shock of knowing my past, my son hates me, my grandchildren are being bullied because of me...I don't deserve anymore love or happiness in life."

"You know I'm not very religious, but I do believe in an existence beyond this one. I also believe in karma and perhaps you have earned back the right to a good life? You could have denied your past, it's unlikely they could have proved you were Ingrid Brecht the camp guard, but you didn't! Listen, perhaps we'll all be judged when we die and then you can explain yourself to whomever. Let's take what time we have left and use it to heal." Anna gripped Ingrid by the shoulders as if to shake some sense into her friend.

Ingrid shook her head. "I love you too, Anna. I missed you so much after the Gestapo took you away. I felt so lost, and stupid without you around. You know I'm no great intellect. I don't know what would have happened to me if you and Herschel had not been a part of my life."

Anna touched Ingrid's face. "Can we please take this very nice conversation back to your house so we can warm up with dry clothes and hot cocoa?"

"Of course, yes!" Ingrid's eyes brightened and she stood up suddenly, slipping on the wet grass and twisting her back.

Not even having time to stand up, Anna watched the shocked expression freeze on Ingrid's features and then she plopped back down the bench, her chin resting on her chest.

"Ingrid, are you okay?' Anna asked knowing that the pellet near Ingrid's spine had moved and severed the spinal cord. With two fingers the doctor found her old best friend's jugular vein and it was still. Ingrid was dead. "Oh God." She dialed emergency services and told them their location just south of the Lionsbridge.

Anna put an arm around her silent friend and sobbed, her heart breaking for the third time as the heavens opened up and wept with her, operatic rounds of lightening and thunderous drum rolls erupting as if heralding the end of an epic drama.

The End

D.A. Chadwick is the author of eleven fiction and nonfiction books. She is a professional translator of French, German and Dutch to English residing in the Midwest, USA.

D.A. Chadwick